THE ETERNAL CHAMPION

MICHAEL MOORCOCK

THE ETERNAL CHAMPION

A FANTASTIC ROMANCE

TITAN BOOKS

The Eternal Champion
Print edition ISBN: 9781783291618
E-book edition ISBN: 9781783291588

Published by Titan Books
A division of Titan Publishing Group Ltd
144 Southwark Street, London SE1 0UP

First edition: November 2014
1 2 3 4 5 6 7 8 9 10

Edited by John Davey

A CIP catalogue record for this title is available from the British Library.

Printed and bound in the United States

To the memory of Douglas Fairbanks,
the greatest hero of them all

THE ETERNAL CHAMPION

ᔕᔕ PROLOGUE ᔕᔕ

THEY CALLED FOR *me.*

That is all I really know.

They called for me and I went to them. I could not do otherwise. The will of the whole of Humanity was a strong thing. It smashed through the ties of time and the chains of space and dragged me to hell.

Why was I chosen? I still do not know, though they believed they had told me. Now it is done and I am here. I shall always be here. And if, as wise men tell me, time is cyclic, then I shall one day return to part of the cycle I knew as the twentieth century, for (it was no wish of mine) I am immortal.

1

A CALL ACROSS TIME

BETWEEN WAKEFULNESS AND sleeping we have most of us had the illusion of hearing voices, scraps of conversation, phrases spoken in unfamiliar tones. Sometimes we attempt to attune our minds so that we can hear more, but we are rarely successful. These illusions are called "hypnagogic hallucinations"—the beginning of the dreams we shall later experience as we sleep.

There was a woman. A child. A city. An occupation. A name: John Daker. A sense of frustration. A need for fulfilment. Though I loved them. I know I loved them.

It was in the winter. I lay miserably in a cold bed and I stared through the window at the moon. I do not remember my exact thoughts. Something to do with morality and the futility of human existence, no doubt. Then, between wakefulness and sleeping, I began every night to hear voices...

At first I dismissed them, expecting to fall immediately asleep, but they continued and I began trying to listen to them, thinking, perhaps, to receive some message from my unconscious. But the most commonly repeated word was gibberish to me:

Erekosë... Erekosë... Erekosë...

I could not recognise the language, though it had a peculiar familiarity. The closest language I could place it with was the language of Sioux Indians, but I knew only a few words of Sioux.

Erekosë... Erekosë... Erekosë...

Each night I redoubled my efforts to concentrate on the voices and gradually I began to experience much stronger hypnagogic hallucinations, until one night it seemed that I broke free from my body altogether.

Had I hung for an eternity in limbo? Was I alive—dead? Was there a memory of a world that lay in the far past or the distant future? Of another world which seemed closer? And the names? Was I John Daker or Erekosë? Was I either of these? Many other names— Corum Jhaelen Irsei, Aubec, Seaton Begg, Elric, Rackhir, Ilian, Oona, Simon, Bastable, Cornelius, the Rose, von Bek, Asquiol, Hawkmoon—fled away down the ghostly rivers of my memory. I hung in darkness, bodiless. A man spoke. Where was he? I tried to look but had no eyes with which to see...

"Erekosë the Champion, where are you?"

Another voice: *"Father... it is only a legend..."*

"No, Iolinda. I feel he is listening. Erekosë..."

I tried to answer, but I had no tongue with which to speak.

Then there were swirling half-dreams of a house in a great city of miracles—a swollen, grimy city of miracles, crammed with dull-coloured machines, many of which bore human passengers. There were buildings, beautiful beneath their coatings of dust, and there were other, brighter buildings not so beautiful, with austere lines and many windows. There were screams and loud noises.

There was a troop of riders galloping over undulating countryside, flamboyant in armour of lacquered gold, coloured pennants draped around their blood-encrusted lances. Their faces were heavy with weariness.

Then there were more faces, many faces. Some of them I half-recognised. Others were completely unfamiliar. Many of these were dressed in strange clothes. I saw a white-haired man in middle age. He wore a tall, spiked crown of iron and diamonds upon his head. His mouth moved. He was speaking…

"Erekosë. It is I—King Rigenos, Defender of Humanity…

"You are needed again, Erekosë. The Hounds of Evil rule a third of the world and humankind is weary with the war against them. Come to us, Erekosë. Lead us to victory. From the Plains of Melting Ice to the Mountains of Sorrow they have set up their corrupt standard and I fear they will advance yet farther into our territories.

"Come to us, Erekosë. Lead us to victory. Come to us, Erekosë. Lead us…"

The woman's voice:

"Father. This is only an empty tomb. Not even the mummy of Erekosë remains. It became drifting dust long ago. Let us leave and return to Necranal to marshal the living peers!"

I felt like a fainting man who strives to fight against dizzy oblivion but, however much he tries, cannot take control of his own brain. Again I tried to answer, but could not.

It was as if I wavered backwards through Time, while every

atom of me wanted to go forward. I had the sensation of vast size, as if I were made of stone with eyelids of granite that measured miles across—eyelids which I could not open.

And then I was tiny: the most minute grain in the universe. And yet I felt I belonged to the whole far more than did the stone giant.

Memories came and went.

The panorama of the twentieth century, its discoveries and its deceits, its beauties and its bitterness, its satisfactions, its strife, its self-delusion, its superstitious fancies to which it gave the name of Science, rushed into my mind like air into a vacuum.

But it was only momentary, for the next second my entire being was flung elsewhere—to a world which was Earth, but not the Earth of John Daker, not quite the world of dead Erekosë...

There were three great continents; two close together were divided from the third by a vast sea containing many islands, large and small.

I saw an ocean of ice which I knew to be slowly shrinking— the Plains of Melting Ice.

I saw the third continent, which bore lush flora, mighty forests, blue lakes and which was bound along its northern coasts by a towering chain of mountains—the Mountains of Sorrow. This I knew to be the domain of the Eldren, whom King Rigenos had called the Hounds of Evil.

Now, on the other two continents, I saw the wheatlands of the West on the continent of Zavara, with their tall cities of multicoloured rock, their rich cities—Stalaco, Calodemia, Mooros, Ninadoon and Dratarda.

There were the great sea-ports—Shilaal, Wedmah, Sinana, Tarkar—and Noonos with her towers cobbled in precious stones.

* * *

Then I saw the fortress cities of the continent of Necralala, with the capital city Necranal chief among them, built on, into and about a mighty mountain, peaked by the spreading palace of its warrior kings.

Now I began to remember as, in the background of my awareness, I heard a voice calling, "*Erekosë, Erekosë, Erekosë…*"

The warrior kings of Necranal, kings for two thousand years of a Humanity united, at war, and united again. The warrior kings of whom King Rigenos was the last living—and ageing now, with only a daughter, Iolinda, to carry on his line. Old and weary with hate—but still hating. Hating the unhuman folk whom he called the Hounds of Evil, mankind's age-old enemies, reckless and wild; linked, it was said, by a thin line of blood to the human race—an outcome of a union between an ancient queen and the Evil One, Azmobaana. Hated by King Rigenos as soulless immortals, slaves of Azmobaana's machinations.

And, hating, he called upon John Daker, whom he named Erekosë, to aid him with his war against them.

"Erekosë, I beg thee answer me. Are you ready to come?" His voice was loud and echoing, and when, after a struggle, I could reply, my own voice seemed to echo, also.

"I am ready," I replied, "but seem to be chained."

"*Chained?*" There was consternation in his voice. "Are you, then, a prisoner of Azmobaana's frightful minions? Are you trapped upon the Ghost Worlds?"

"Perhaps," I said. "But I do not think so. It is Space and Time which chain me. I am separated from you by a gulf without form or dimension."

"How may we bridge that gulf and bring you to us?"

"The united wills of Humanity may serve the purpose."

"Already we pray that you may come to us."

"Then continue," I said.

I was falling away again. I thought I remembered laughter, sadness, pride. Then, suddenly, more faces. I felt as if I witnessed the passing of everyone I had known, down the ages, and then one face superimposed itself over the others—the head and shoulders of an amazingly beautiful woman, with blonde hair piled beneath a diadem of precious stones which seemed to light the sweetness of her oval face. "Iolinda," I said.

I saw her more solidly now. She was clinging to the arm of the tall, gaunt man who wore the crown of iron and diamonds: King Rigenos.

They stood before an empty platform of quartz and gold and resting on a cushion of dust was a straight sword which they dared not touch. Neither did they dare step too close to it, for it gave off a radiation which might slay them.

It was a tomb in which they stood.

The tomb of Erekosë. My tomb.

I moved towards the platform, hanging over it.

Ages before, my body had been placed there. I stared at the sword, which held no dangers for me, but I was unable in my captivity to pick it up. It was my spirit only which inhabited that dark place—but the whole of my spirit now, not the fragment which had inhabited the tomb for thousands of years. That fragment had heard King Rigenos and had enabled John Daker to hear it, to come to it, to be united with it.

* * *

"Erekosë!" called the king, straining his eyes through the gloom as if he had seen me. "Erekosë! We pray."

Then I experienced the dreadful pain which I supposed must be like that of a woman experiencing childbirth, a pain that seemed eternal and yet was intrinsically its own vanquisher. I was screaming, writhing in the air above them. Great spasms of agony—but an agony complete with purpose—the purpose of creation.

I shrieked. But there was joy in my cry.

I groaned. But there was triumph there.

I grew heavy and I reeled. I grew heavier and heavier and I gasped, stretching out my arms to balance myself.

I had flesh and I had muscle and I had blood and I had strength. The strength coursed through me and I took a huge breath and touched my body. It was a powerful body, tall and fit.

I looked up. I stood before them in the flesh. I was their god and I had returned.

"I have come," I said. "I am here, King Rigenos. I have left nothing worthwhile behind me, but do not let me regret that leaving."

"You will not regret it, Champion." He was pale, exhilarated, smiling. I looked at Iolinda, who dropped her eyes modestly and then, as if against her will, raised them again to regard me. I turned to the dais on my right.

"My sword," I said, reaching for it.

I heard King Rigenos sigh with satisfaction.

"They are doomed now, the dogs," he said.

∽ 2 ∼

"THE CHAMPION HAS COME!"

THEY HAD A sheath for the sword. It had been made days before. King Rigenos left to get it, leaving me alone with his daughter.

Now that I was here, I did not think to question how I came and why it should have been possible. Neither, it seemed, did she question the fact. I was there. It seemed inevitable.

We regarded one another silently until the king returned with the scabbard.

"This will protect us against your sword's poison," he said.

He held it out to me. For a moment I hesitated before stretching my own hand towards it and accepting it.

The king frowned and looked at the ground. Then he folded his arms across his chest.

I held the scabbard in my two hands. It was opaque, like old glass, but the metal was unfamiliar to me—or rather to John Daker. It was light, flexible and strong.

I turned and picked up the sword. The handle was bound in gold thread and was vibrant to my touch. The pommel was a globe of deep red onyx and the hilt was worked in strips of silver and black onyx. The blade was long and straight and sharp, but it did not shine like steel. Instead, in colour, it resembled lead. The sword was beautifully balanced and I swung it through the air and laughed aloud, and it seemed to laugh with me.

"Erekosë! Sheathe it!" cried King Rigenos in alarm. "Sheathe it! The radiation is death to all but yourself!"

I was reluctant now to put the sword away. The feel of it awakened a dim remembrance.

"Erekosë! Please! I beg you!" Iolinda's voice echoed her father's. "Sheathe the sword!"

Reluctantly I slid the sword into its scabbard. Why was I the only one who could wear the sword without being affected by its radiation?

Was it because, in that transition from my own age to this, I had become constitutionally different in some way? Was it that the ancient Erekosë and the unborn John Daker (or was it vice versa?) had metabolisms which had adapted to protect themselves against the power which flowed from the sword?

I shrugged. It did not matter. The fact itself was enough. I was unconcerned. It was as if I was aware that my fate had been taken almost entirely out of my own hands. I had become a tool.

If only I had known then to what use the tool would be put, then I might have fought against the pull and remained the harmless intellectual, John Daker. But perhaps I could not have fought and won. The power that drew me to this age was very great.

At any rate, I was prepared at that moment to do whatever Fate demanded of me. I stood where I had materialised, in the tomb of Erekosë, and I revelled in my strength and in my sword.

Later, things were to change.

* * *

"I will need clothes," I said, for I was naked. "And armour. And a steed. I am Erekosë."

"Clothes have been prepared," said King Rigenos. He clapped his hands. "Here."

The slaves entered. One carried a robe, another a cloak, another a white cloth which I gathered had to serve for underwear. They wrapped the cloth around my lower quarters and slipped the robe over my head. It was loose and cool and felt pleasant on my skin. It was deep blue, with complicated designs stitched into it in gold, silver and scarlet thread. The cloak was scarlet, with designs of gold, silver and blue. They gave me soft boots of doeskin to put on my feet, and a wide belt of light brown leather with an iron buckle in which were set rubies and sapphires, and I hung my scabbard on this. Then I gripped the sword with my left fist.

"I am ready," I said.

Iolinda shuddered. "Then let us leave this gloomy place," she murmured.

With one last look back at the dais on which the heap of dust still lay, I walked with the King and the Princess of Necranal out of my own tomb and into a calm day that, while warm, had a light breeze blowing. We were standing on a small hill. Behind us the tomb, apparently built of black quartz, looked time-worn and ancient, pitted by the passing of many storms and many winds. On its roof was the corroded statue of a warrior mounted on a great battle charger. The face had been smoothed by dust and rain, but I knew it. It was my face.

I looked away.

Below us a caravan was waiting. There were the richly caparisoned horses and a guard of men dressed in that same golden armour I had seen in my dreams. These warriors, however, were fresher-looking than the others. Their armour was fluted, embellished with raised designs, ornate and beautiful but, according to my sparse reading on the subject of armour, coupled with Erekosë's stirring memory, totally unsuitable for war. The fluting and embossing acted as a trap to catch the point of a spear or sword, whereas armour should be made to turn a point. This armour, for all its beauty, acted more as an extra danger than a protection.

The guards were mounted on heavy warhorses, but the beasts that knelt awaiting us resembled a kind of camel from which all the camel's lumpen ugliness had been bred. These beasts were beautiful. On their high backs were cabins of ebony, ivory and mother-of-pearl, curtained in scintillating silks.

We walked down the hill and, as we walked, I noticed that I still had on my finger the ring that I had worn as John Daker, a ring of woven silver that my wife had given me. My wife—I could not recall her face. I felt I should have left the ring behind me, on that other body. But perhaps there is no body left behind.

We reached the kneeling beasts and the guards stiffened their backs to acknowledge our arrival. I saw curiosity in many of the eyes that looked at me.

King Rigenos gestured towards one of the beasts. "Would you care to take your cabin, Champion?" Though he himself had summoned me, he seemed to be slightly wary of me.

"Thank you." I climbed the little ladder of plaited silk and entered the cabin. It was completely lined with deep cushions of a variety of hues.

The camels climbed to their feet and we began to move swiftly through a narrow valley whose sides were lined with evergreen trees which I could not name—something like spreading monkey-puzzle trees, but with more branches and broader leaves.

I had laid my sword across my knees. I inspected it. It was a plain soldier's sword, having no markings on the blade. The hilt fitted perfectly into my right hand as I gripped it. It was a good sword. But why it was poisonous to others I did not know. Presumably it was also lethal to those whom King Rigenos called the Hounds of Evil—the Eldren.

As we travelled through the soft day I drowsed on my cushions, feeling strangely weary, until I heard a cry and pushed back the curtains of my cabin to look ahead.

There was Necranal, the city which I had seen in my dreams.

Far away still, it towered upwards so that the entire mountain upon which it was built was hidden by its wondrous architecture. Minarets, steeples, domes and battlements shone in the sun and above them all loomed the huge palace of the warrior kings, a noble structure, many-towered, the Palace of Ten Thousand Windows. I remembered the name.

I saw King Rigenos peer from his own cabin and cry: "Katorn! Ride ahead and tell the people that Erekosë the Champion has come to drive the Evil Ones back to the Mountains of Sorrow!"

The man he addressed was a sullen-faced individual, doubtless the Captain of the Imperial Guard. "Aye, sire," he growled.

He drew his horse out of line and galloped speedily along the road of white dust which wound now down an incline. I could see the road stretching for many miles into the distance towards Necranal. I watched the rider for a while but wearied of this eventually and instead strained my eyes to make out details in that great city structure.

The cities of London, New York or Tokyo were probably bigger in area, but not much. Necranal was spread around the base of the mountain for many miles. Surrounding the city was a high wall upon which turrets were mounted at intervals.

So, at last, we came to the great main gate of Necranal and our caravan halted.

A musical instrument sounded and the gates began to swing open. We passed through into streets packed with jostling, cheering people who shouted so loudly I was forced, at times, to cover my ears for fear they would rupture.

3

THE ELDREN THREAT

Now THE CHEERING gradually fell away as the little caravan ascended the winding road to the Palace of Ten Thousand Windows. A silence settled and I heard only the creak of the howdah in which I sat, the occasional jingle of harness or the clatter of a horse's hoof. I began to feel discomfited. There was something about the mood of the city that was not altogether sane and which could not be explained away in conventional terms. Certainly the people were afraid of enemy attack; certainly they were weary with fighting. But it seemed to me that this mood held something morbid—a mixture of hysterical elation and melancholic depression that I had sensed only once before in my previous life, during my single visit to a mental hospital.

Or perhaps I was merely imposing my own mood on my surroundings. After all, it could be argued that I was experiencing classic paranoid-schizophrenic symptoms! A man with two or more well-defined identities who also happened to be considered in this world the potential saviour of mankind! For a moment I wondered if in fact I had not gone completely insane, if this were not some monstrous delusion, if I were not *actually* at this moment in the very madhouse I had once visited!

I touched the draperies, my scabbarded sword; I peered out at the vast city now stretched out below me; I stared at the huge bulk of the Palace of Ten Thousand Windows above me. I attempted to see beyond them, deliberately assuming that they were an illusion, expecting to see the walls of a hospital room, or even the familiar walls of my own apartment. But the Palace of Ten Thousand Windows remained as solid as ever. The city of Necranal had none of the qualities of a mirage. I sank back in my cushions. I had to assume that this was real, that I had been transported somehow across the ages and through space to this Earth of which there were no records in any history book I had ever read (and I had read many) and of which there were only echoes in myths and legends.

I was no longer John Daker. I was Erekosë—the Eternal Champion.

A legend myself, come to life.

I laughed then. If I were mad, then it was a glorious madness, a madness which I would never have considered myself capable of inventing!

At length our caravan arrived at the summit of the mountain and the jewelled gates of the palace opened for us and we passed inside a splendid courtyard in which trees grew and fountains played, feeding little rivers spanned by ornamental bridges. Fish swam in the rivers and birds sang in the trees as pages came forward to make our beasts kneel down and we stepped out into the evening light.

King Rigenos smiled with pride as he gestured around the great courtyard. "You like this, Erekosë? I had it built myself, shortly after I came to the throne. The courtyard was a gloomy sort of place until then—it did not fit with the rest of the palace."

"It is very beautiful," I said. I turned to look at Iolinda, who had joined us. "And not the only beautiful thing you have helped create—for here is the most beautiful adornment to your palace!"

King Rigenos chuckled. "You are a courtier as well as a warrior, I see." He took my arm and Iolinda's and guided us across the courtyard. "Of course, I have little time these days to consider the creation of beauty. It is weapons we must create now. Instead of plans for gardens, I must concern myself with battle plans." He sighed. "Perhaps you will drive the Eldren away for ever, Erekosë. Perhaps, when they are destroyed, we shall be able to enjoy the peaceful things of life again."

I felt sorry for him at that moment. He only wanted what every man wanted—freedom from fear, a chance to raise children with a reasonable certainty that they would be allowed to do the same, a chance to look forward to the future without the knowledge that any plans made might be wrecked for ever by some sudden act of violence. His world, after all, was not so different from the one I had so recently left.

I put my hand on the king's shoulder. "Let us hope so, King Rigenos," I said. "I will do what I can."

He cleared his throat. "And that will be a great deal, Champion. I know it will be a great deal. We shall soon rid ourselves of the Eldren menace!"

We entered a cool hall whose walls were lined with beaten silver over which tapestries were draped. It was a pleasant hall, though very large. Off the hall led a wide staircase and down the staircase now descended a whole army of slaves, servants and retainers of all kinds. They drew themselves up in ranks at the bottom and knelt to greet the king.

"This is Lord Erekosë," King Rigenos told them. "He is a great warrior and my honoured guest. Treat him as you would treat me—obey him as you would obey me. All that he wishes shall be his."

To my embarrassment, the assemblage fell to its knees again and chorused: "Greetings, Lord Erekosë."

I spread my hands. They rose. I was beginning to take this sort of behaviour for granted. There was no doubt that part of me was used to it.

"I shall not burden you with ceremony for tonight," Rigenos said. "If you would like to refresh yourself in the apartments we have set aside for your use, we shall visit you later."

"Very well," I said. I turned to Iolinda and put out my hand to take hers. She extended it after a moment's hesitation and I kissed it. "I look forward to seeing you both again in a little time," I murmured, looking deep into her marvellous eyes. She dropped her gaze and withdrew her hand, and I allowed the servants to escort me upstairs to my apartments.

Twenty large rooms had been set aside for my use. These contained quarters for a staff of some ten personal slaves and servants and they were most of them extravagantly furnished with an eye to luxury that, it seemed to me, the people of the twentieth century had lost. "Opulent" was the word that sprang to mind. I could not move but a slave would come forward and take my surcoat or help me pour a glass of water or arrange the cushions of a divan. Yet I was still somewhat uneasy and it was a relief, on exploring the apartments, to come upon more austere rooms. These were weapon-lined warriors' rooms, without cushions or silks or furs, but with solid benches and blades and maces of iron and steel, brass-shod lances and razor-sharp arrows.

I spent some time in the weapons rooms and then returned to eat. My slaves brought me food and wine and I ate and drank heartily.

When I had finished, I felt as if I had been asleep for a long time and had awakened invigorated. Again I paced the rooms, exploring them further, taking more interest in the weapons than in the furnishings, which would have delighted even the most jaded sybarite. I stepped out onto one of the several covered balconies and surveyed the great city of Necranal as the sun set over it and deep shadows began to flow through the streets.

The faraway sky was full of smoky colour. There were purples, oranges, yellows and blues and these colours were reflected in the domes and steeples of Necranal so that the entire city seemed to take on a softer texture, like a pastel drawing.

The shadows grew blacker. The sun set and stained the topmost domes scarlet and then night fell and fire flared suddenly all around the distant walls of Necranal, the yellow and red flames leaping upward at intervals of a few yards and illuminating much of the city within the walls. Lights appeared in windows and I heard the calls of nightbirds and insects. I turned to go in and saw that my servants had lit lamps for me. It had grown colder, but I hesitated on the balcony and decided to stay where I was, thinking deeply about my strange situation and trying to gauge the exact nature of the perils which Humanity faced.

There came a sound behind me. I looked back into the apartments and saw King Rigenos entering. Moody Katorn, Captain of the Imperial Guard, was with him. Instead of a helmet, he now wore a platinum circlet on his head and, instead of a breastplate, a leather jerkin stamped with a design in gold, but the absence of armour did not seem to soften his general demeanour. King Rigenos was wrapped in a white fur cloak and still wore his spiked crown of iron and diamonds. The two men joined me on the balcony.

"You feel rested, I hope, Erekosë?" King Rigenos enquired

almost nervously, as if he had expected me to fade into air while he was away.

"I feel very well, thank you, King Rigenos."

"Good." He hesitated.

"Time is valuable," Katorn grunted.

"Yes, Katorn. Yes, I know." King Rigenos looked at me as if he hoped I already knew what he wished to say, but I did not and could only stare back, waiting for him to speak.

"You will forgive us, Erekosë," said Katorn, "if we come immediately to the matter of the Human Kingdoms. The king would outline to you our position and what we require of you."

"Of course," I said. "I am ready." I was in fact very anxious to learn the position.

"We have maps," said King Rigenos. "Where are the maps, Katorn?"

"Within, sire."

"Shall we…?"

I nodded and we entered my apartments. We passed through two chambers until we came to the main living room, in which was a large oak table. Here stood several of King Rigenos's slaves with large rolls of parchment under their arms. Katorn selected several of the rolls and spread them, one on top of the other, on the table. He drew his heavy dagger to weight one side and picked up a metal vase studded with rubies and emeralds to hold the other side.

I looked at the maps with interest. I already recognised them. I had seen something similar in my dreams before I had been called here by King Rigenos's incantations.

Now the king bent over the maps and his long, pale index finger traced over the territories shown.

"As I told you in your—your tomb, Erekosë, the Eldren now dominate the entire southern continent. They call this continent

Mernadin. There." His finger now hovered over a coastal region of the continent. "Five years ago they recaptured the only real outpost we had on Mernadin. Here. Their ancient sea-port of Paphanaal. There was little fighting."

"Your forces fled?" I asked.

Katorn came in again. "I admit that we had grown complacent. When they suddenly swept out of the Mountains of Sorrow, we were unprepared. They must have been building their damned armies for years and we were unaware of it. We could not be expected to know their plans—they're aided by sorcery and we are not!"

"You were able to evacuate most of your colonies, I take it?" I put in.

Katorn shrugged. "There was little evacuation necessary. Mernadin was virtually uninhabited since human beings would not live in a land which had been polluted by the presence of the Hounds of Evil. The continent is cursed. Inhabited by fiends from Hell."

I rubbed my chin and asked innocently: "Then why did you drive the Eldren back to the mountains in the first place if you had no need of their territories?"

"Because, while they had the land under their control, they were a constant threat to Humanity!"

"I see." I made a tiny gesture with my right hand. "Forgive me for interrupting you. Please continue."

"A constant threat—" began Katorn.

"That threat is once again imminent," the king's voice broke in. It was thick and trembling. His eyes were suddenly full of fear and hatred. "We expect them at any moment to launch an attack upon the Two Continents—upon Zavara and Necralala!"

"Do you know when they plan this invasion?" I asked. "How long have we to ready ourselves?"

"They'll attack!" Katorn's bleak eyes came to life. The thin beard framing his pale face seemed to bristle.

"They'll attack," agreed King Rigenos. "They would have overrun us now if we did not constantly war against them."

"We have to keep them back," added Katorn. "Once a breach is made, they will engulf us!"

King Rigenos sighed. "Humanity, though, is battle-weary. We needed one of two things—though ideally both—fresh warriors to drive the Eldren back or a leader to give the warriors we have new hope."

"And you can train no fresh warriors?" I asked.

Katorn made a short, guttural sound in his throat. I took this to be a laugh. "Impossible! All mankind fights the Eldren menace!"

The king nodded. "So I called you, Erekosë—though believing myself to be a desperate fool willing to think a mirage reality."

Katorn turned away at this. It seemed to me that this had been his private theory—that the king had gone mad in his desperation. My materialization seemed to have destroyed this theory and made him in some way resentful of me, though I did not think I could be blamed for the king's decision.

The king straightened his shoulders. "I called you. And I hold you to your vow."

I knew of no vow. I was surprised. "What vow?" I said.

Now the king looked astonished. "Why, the vow that, if ever the Eldren dominated Mernadin again, you would come to decide the struggle between them and Humanity."

"I see." I signed to a slave to bring me a cup of wine and I sipped it and stared at the map. As John Daker, I saw a meaningless war between two ferocious, blindly hating factions, both of whom seemed to be conducting a racial jihad, one against the other. Yet my loyalties were clear. I belonged to the human race and should use all my powers to help defend my kind. Humanity had to be saved.

"The Eldren?" I looked up at King Rigenos. "What do they say?"

"What do you mean?" Katorn growled. "*Say*? You speak as if you do not believe our king."

"I am not questioning the truth of your statements," I told him. "I wish to know the exact terms in which the Eldren justify their war against us. It would help if I had a clearer idea of their ambitions."

Katorn shrugged. "They would wipe us out," he said. "Is that not enough to know?"

"No," I said. "You must have taken prisoners. What do the prisoners tell you?" I spread my hands. "How have the Eldren leaders justified their war against Humanity?"

King Rigenos smiled patronizingly. "You have forgotten a great deal, Erekosë, if you have forgotten the Eldren. They are not human. They are clever. They are cold and they have smooth, deceitful tongues with which they would lull a man into a false sense of tranquility before tearing his heart from his body with their bare fangs. They are brave, though, I'll give them that. Under torture they die, refusing to tell us their true plans. They are cunning. They try to make us believe their talk of peace, of mutual trust and mutual help, hoping that we will drop our defences long enough so that they may turn and destroy us, or get us to look them full in the face so that they can work the evil eye upon us. Do not be naïve, Erekosë. Do not attempt to deal with an Eldren as you would deal with a human being, for if you did so, you would be doomed. They have no souls, as we understand souls. They have no love, save a cold loyalty to their cause and to their master Azmobaana. Realise this, Erekosë—the Eldren are demons. They are fiends to whom Azmobaana in his dreadful blasphemy has granted something like a human form. But you must not be blinded by the form. That which is inside an Eldren is *not* human—it is everything, in fact, that is unhuman."

Katorn's face twisted.

"You cannot trust an Eldren wolf. They are treacherous, immoral and evil. We shall not be safe until their whole race is destroyed. Utterly destroyed—so that not a fragment of their flesh, not a droplet of their blood, not a splinter of their bone, not a strand of their hair is left to taint the Earth. And I speak literally, Erekosë, for whilst one finger-clipping of an Eldren survives upon our world, then there is the chance that Azmobaana can re-create his servants and attack us again. That demon brood must be burned to the finest ash—every man, every female and every youngling. Burned—then cast to the winds, the clean winds. That is our mission, Erekosë, the mission of Humanity. And we have the Good One's blessing for that mission."

Then I heard another voice, a sweeter voice, and I glanced towards the door. It was Iolinda.

"You must lead us to victory, Erekosë," she said candidly. "What Katorn says is true—no matter how fiercely he declaims it. The facts are as he tells you. You must lead us to victory."

I looked again into her eyes. I drew a deep breath and my face felt hard and cold.

"I will lead you," I said.

4

IOLINDA

THE NEXT MORNING I awoke to the sounds of the slaves preparing my breakfast. Or was it the slaves? Was it not my wife moving about the room, getting ready to wake up the boy as she did every morning?

I opened my eyes expecting to see her.

I did not see her. Nor did I see my room in my apartment where I had lived as John Daker.

Nor did I see slaves.

Instead, I saw Iolinda. She was smiling down at me as she prepared the breakfast with her own hands.

I felt guilty for a moment, as if I had betrayed my wife in some obscure way. Then I realised that there was nothing I could be ashamed of. I was the victim of Fate—of forces which I could not hope to understand. I was not John Daker. I was Erekosë. I realised that it would be the best for me if I were to insist on that. A man divided between two identities is a sick man. I resolved to forget John Daker as soon as possible. Since I was Erekosë now, I should concentrate on being Erekosë only. In that I was a fatalist.

Iolinda brought a bowl of fruit towards me. "Would you eat, Lord Erekosë?"

I selected a strange, soft fruit with a reddish yellow skin. She handed me a small knife. I tried to peel it, but since the fruit was new to me, I was not sure how to begin. She gently took it from me and began to peel it for me, sitting on the edge of my low bed and concentrating rather excessively, in my opinion, on the fruit she held.

At last the fruit was peeled and she quartered it and placed it on a plate and handed the plate to me, still avoiding my direct gaze, but smiling a little mysteriously as she looked about her. I picked up a piece of the fruit and bit it. It was sharp and sweet at the same time and very refreshing.

"Thank you," I said. "It is good. I have never had this fruit before."

"Have you not?" She was genuinely surprised. "But the *ecrex* is the commonest fruit in Necralala."

"You forget I am a stranger to Necralala," I pointed out.

She put her head on one side and looked at me with a slight frown. She pushed back the flimsy blue cloth that covered her golden hair and made a great play of arranging her matching blue gown. She really did seem to be puzzled. "A stranger..." she murmured.

"A stranger," I agreed.

"But—" she paused— "but you are the great hero of Humanity, Lord Erekosë. You knew Necranal as it was in its greatest glory—when you ruled here as the Champion. You knew Earth in ancient times, when you set it free from the chains the Eldren had bound around it. You know more of this world than I do, Erekosë."

I shrugged. "I admit that much of it is familiar—and growing increasingly familiar. But until yesterday my name was John Daker and I lived in a city very different from Necranal and my occupation was not that of warrior or, indeed, anything like it. I do not deny that I am Erekosë—the name is familiar and I am comfortable with it. But I do not know *who* Erekosë was, any more than do you. He was a great hero of ancient times who, before he died, swore that he would return to decide the issue between Eldren and Humanity if he were needed. He was placed in a rather gloomy tomb on a hillside along with his sword, which only he could wield."

"The sword Kanajana," murmured Iolinda.

"It has a name, then?"

"Aye—Kanajana. It—it is more than a name, I believe. It is some sort of mystic description—a description of its exact nature—of the powers it contains."

"And is there any legend that explains why only I can bear that blade?" I asked her.

"There are several," she said.

"Which do you prefer?" I smiled.

Then, for the first time that morning, she looked directly at me and her voice lowered and she said: "I prefer the one that says that you are the chosen son of the Good One, the Great One— that your sword is a sword of the gods and that you can handle it because you are a god—an Immortal."

I laughed. "You do not believe that?"

She dropped her gaze. "If you tell me that it is not true, then I must believe you," she said. "Of course."

"I admit that I feel extremely healthy," I told her. "But that is a long way from feeling as a god must feel! Besides, I think I would know if I were a god. I would know other gods. I would dwell in some plane where the gods dwell. I would count goddesses amongst my friends." I stopped. She seemed disturbed.

I reached out and touched her and said softly: "But then perhaps you are right. Perhaps I am a god—for I am certainly privileged to know a goddess."

She shrugged off my hand. "You are making mock of me, my lord."

"No. I swear it."

She got up. "I must appear foolish to such a great lord as yourself. I apologise for wasting your time with my chatter."

"You have not wasted my time," I said. "You have helped me, in fact."

Her lips parted. "Helped you?"

"Yes. You have filled in part of my somewhat peculiar background. I still do not remember my past as Erekosë, but at least I know as much about that past as anyone here. Which is not a disadvantage!"

"Perhaps your centuries-long sleep has washed your mind free of memory," she said.

"Perhaps," I agreed. "Or perhaps there have been so many other memories during that sleep—new experiences, other lives."

"What do you mean?"

"Well, it seems to me that I have been more people than just John Daker and Erekosë. Other names spring to mind—strange names in unfamiliar tongues. I have a vague—and perhaps stupid—notion that while I slept as Erekosë, my spirit took on other shapes and names. Some in the future, some in the past, some—elsewhere..." I could not explain, but added lamely: "Perhaps that spirit cannot sleep, but must for ever be active." I stopped. I was getting deep into the realms of metaphysics—and I had never possessed any great predilection for metaphysics. I considered myself a pragmatist, in fact. Such notions as reincarnation I had always scoffed at—still scoffed at, really, in spite of the evidence, such as it was.

But Iolinda pressed me to continue what I considered to be pointless speculation. "Go on," she said. "Please continue, Lord Erekosë."

If only to keep the beautiful girl beside me for a short while longer, I did as she asked.

"Well," I said, "while you and your father were attempting to bring me here, I thought I remembered other lives than this one as Erekosë or the other one, as John Daker. I remembered, very dimly, other civilizations—though I could not tell you whether they existed in the past or in the future. In fact, the idea of past and future seems meaningless to me now. I have no idea, for instance, whether this civilization lies in the 'future' that I know as John Daker or in the 'past'. It is here. I am here. Perhaps there is only ever 'the present'? There are certain things that I will have to do. That is all I can say."

"But these other incarnations," she said. "What do you know of them?"

I shrugged. "Nothing. I am attempting to describe a dim feeling, not an exact impression. A few names which I have now forgotten. A few images which have almost completely faded away as dreams fade. And perhaps that is all they ever were— just dreams. Perhaps my life as John Daker, which in its turn is beginning to fade in my memory, was merely that, a dream. Certainly I know nothing of any supernatural agencies of whom your father and Katorn have spoken. I know of no 'Azmobaana', no Good and Great One, no demons or, indeed, angels. I know only that I am a man and that I exist."

Her face was grave. "That is true. You are a man. You exist. I saw you materialise."

"But from where did I come?"

"From the Other Regions," she said. "From the place where all great warriors go when they die, and where their women go to join them, to live in eternal happiness."

Again I smiled, but then smothered the smile for I did not wish to offend her beliefs. "I remember no such place," I said. "I remember only strife. If I have been away from here, it was not in some land of eternal happiness—it was in many lands, lands of eternal warfare."

Suddenly I felt depressed and weary. "Eternal warfare," I repeated and I sighed.

Her look became sympathetic. "Do you think that this is your fate—to war for ever against the enemies of Humanity?"

I frowned. "Not quite, for I seem to remember times when I was not human as you would understand the word. If I have a spirit, as I said, that inhabits many forms, then there have been times when it has inhabited forms that were—different." I rejected the thought. It was too difficult to grasp, too frightening to tolerate.

It disturbed Iolinda. She rose and darted a look of incomprehension at me. "Not—not as an…"

I smiled. "An Eldren? I do not know. But I do not think so, for the name is not familiar to me in that respect."

She was relieved. "It is so hard to trust…" she said sadly.

"To trust what? Words?"

"To trust anything," she said. "I once thought I understood the world. Perhaps I was too young. Now I understand nothing. I do not know whether I shall even be alive next year."

"I think that may be described as a common fear to all we mortals," I said gently.

"'We mortals'?" Her smile was without humour. "You are not mortal, Erekosë!"

I had not up to now considered it. After all, I had been summoned into existence in thin air! I laughed. "We shall soon know whether I am or not," I said, "when we have joined battle with the Eldren!"

A little moan escaped her lips then. "Oh!" she cried. "Do not consider it!" She moved towards the door. "You *are* immortal, Erekosë! You *are* invulnerable! You *are*—eternal! You are the only thing of which I can be sure, the only person I can trust! Do not joke so! Do not joke so, I beg you!"

I was astonished at this outburst. I would have risen from the bed to hold her and comfort her, but I was naked. Admittedly she had seen me naked once before, when I had originally materialised in Erekosë's tomb, but I did not know enough of the customs of these people to guess whether it would shock her or not.

"Forgive me, Iolinda," I said. "I did not realise…"

What had I not realised? The extent of the poor girl's insecurity? Or something deeper than that?

"Do not go," I begged.

She stopped by the door and turned, and there were tears in her huge, wide eyes. "You are eternal, Erekosë. You are immortal. You can never die!"

I could not reply.

For all I knew I would be dead in the first encounter with the Eldren.

Suddenly I became aware of the responsibility I had tacitly agreed to assume—a responsibility not just to this beautiful woman but to the whole human race. I swallowed hard and fell back on my pillows as Iolinda rushed from the room.

Could I possibly bear such a burden?

Did I wish to bear such a burden?

I did not. I had no great faith in my own powers and there was no reason to believe that those powers were any more potent than, say, Katorn's. Katorn was, after all, far more experienced in warfare than I. He had a right to be resentful of me. I had taken over his rôle, robbed him of his power and of a responsibility which he had been prepared to shoulder— and I was unproven. Suddenly I saw Katorn's point of view and sympathised with it.

What right had I to lead Humanity in a war that could decide its very existence?

None.

And then another thought came to me—a more self-pitying thought.

What right had Humanity to expect so much of me?

They had, let us say, awakened me from a slumber which I had earned, leading the quiet, decent life of John Daker. And now they were imposing their will upon me, demanding that I give back to them the self-confidence and—yes—self-righteousness that they were losing.

I lay there in the bed and for a while I hated King Rigenos, Katorn and the rest of the human race—including the fair Iolinda, who had been the one to bring this question to my mind.

Erekosë the Champion, Defender of Humanity, Greatest of Warriors, lay wretched and snivelling in his bed and felt very sorry for himself indeed.

5

KATORN

I AROSE AT last and dressed myself in a simple tunic, having been washed and shaved—much to my embarrassment—by my slaves. I went by myself into the weapons rooms and there took down my sword from where it hung in its scabbard on a peg.

I unsheathed the blade and again a sort of exultation filled me. Immediately I forgot my qualms and scruples and laughed as the sword whistled around my head and my muscles flexed with the weight of it.

I feinted with the sword and it seemed that it was part of my very body, that it was another limb whose presence I had been unaware of until now. I thrust it out at full reach, pulled it back, swung it down. It filled me with joy to wield it!

It made me into something greater than I had ever felt I was before. It made me into a man. A warrior. A champion.

And yet, as John Daker, I had handled swords perhaps twice in my life—and handled them most clumsily, according to those friends of mine who had considered themselves experts.

At last I reluctantly sheathed the sword as I saw a slave hovering some distance away. I remembered that only I, Erekosë, could hold the sword and live.

"What is it?" I said.

"The Lord Katorn, master. He would speak with you."

I put my sword back on its peg. "Bid him enter," I told the slave.

Katorn came in rapidly. He appeared to have been waiting some time and was in no better a mood than when I had first encountered him. His boots, which seemed to be shod with metal, clattered on the flagstones of the weapons room.

"Good morning to you, Lord Erekosë," he said.

I bowed. "Good morning, Lord Katorn. I apologise if you were made to wait. I was trying out that sword."

"The sword Kanajana." Katorn looked at it speculatively.

"The sword Kanajana," I said. "Would you have some refreshment, Lord Katorn?" I was making a great effort to please him, not only because it would not do to have so experienced a warrior as an enemy when plans of battle were being prepared, but because I had, as I said, come to sympathise with his situation.

But Katorn refused to be mollified. "I broke my fast at dawn," he said. "I have come to discuss more pressing matters than eating, Lord Erekosë."

"And what are those?" Manfully I restrained my own temper.

"Matters of war, Lord Erekosë. What else?"

"Indeed. And what specific matters would you wish to discuss with me, Lord Katorn?"

"It seems to me that we should attack the Eldren before they come against us."

"Attack being the best form of defence, eh?"

He looked surprised at this. He had plainly not heard the phrase before. "Eloquently put, my lord. One would think you an Eldren yourself, with such a way with words." He was deliberately trying my temper. But I swallowed the insinuation.

"So," I said, "we attack them. Where?"

"That is what we shall have to discuss with all those concerned in planning this war. But it seems there is one obvious point."

"And that is?"

He wheeled and strode into another chamber, returning with a map which he spread on a bench. It was a map of Mernadin, the third continent, the one entirely controlled by the Eldren. With his dagger he stabbed at a spot I had seen indicated the night before.

"Paphanaal," I said.

"While it is the logical point of an initial attack in a campaign of the sort we plan, it seems to me unlikely that the Eldren will expect us to make so bold a move, knowing that we are weary and under strength."

"But if we are weary and weak," I said, "would it not seem a good idea to attack some less important city first?"

"You are forgetting, my lord, that our warriors have been heartened by your coming," Katorn said dryly.

I could not help grinning at this cut. But Katorn scowled, angry that I had not taken offence.

I said quietly: "We must learn to work together, my lord Katorn. I bow to your great experience as a warrior leader. I acknowledge that you have had much more recent knowledge of the Eldren than have I. I need your help surely as much as King Rigenos believes he needs mine."

Katorn seemed slightly comforted by this. He cleared his throat and continued.

"Once Paphanaal, province *and* city, are taken, we shall have a beachhead from which other attacks inland can be made. With Paphanaal again in our hands, we can decide our own strategy—initiate action rather than react to the Eldren's strategy. Only once we have pushed them back into the mountains will we have the wearying task of clearing them all out. It will take years. But it is what we should have done in the first place. That, however, will be a matter for ordinary military administration and will not concern us directly."

"And what kind of defences has Paphanaal?" I asked.

Katorn smiled. "She relies almost entirely on her warships. If we can destroy her fleet, then Paphanaal is as good as taken." He bared his teeth in what I gathered was a grin. And he looked at me, his expression changing to one of sudden suspicion, as if he had revealed too much to me.

I could not ignore the expression. "What is on your mind, Lord Katorn?" I asked. "Do you not trust me?"

He controlled his features. "I must trust you," he said flatly. "We all must trust you, Lord Erekosë. Have you not returned to fulfil your ancient promise?"

I gazed searchingly into his face. "Do you believe that?"

"I must believe it."

"Do you believe that I am Erekosë the Champion returned?"

"I must believe that also."

"You believe it because you surmise that, if I am not Erekosë—the Erekosë of the legends—then Humanity is doomed?"

He lowered his head as if in assent.

"And what if I am not Erekosë, my lord?"

Katorn looked up. "You must be Erekosë—my lord. If it were not for one thing, I would suspect…"

"What would you suspect?"

"Nothing."

"You would suspect that I were an Eldren in disguise. Is that it, Lord Katorn? Some cunning unhuman who had assumed the outer appearance of a man? Do I read your thoughts correctly, my lord?"

"Too correctly." Katorn's thick brows came together and his mouth was thin and white. "The Eldren are said to have the power to probe minds. But human beings do not possess that power."

"And are you, then, afraid, Lord Katorn?"

"Of an Eldren? By the Good One, I'll show you…" and Katorn's heavy hand rushed to the hilt of his sword.

I raised my own hand and then pointed at the sword that hung sheathed on the peg on the wall. "But that is the one fact that does not fit your theory, isn't it? If I am not Erekosë, then how is it that I can handle Erekosë's blade?"

He did not draw his sword, but his grip remained on the hilt.

"It is true, is it not, that no living creature—human or Eldren—can touch that blade and live?" I said quietly.

"That is the legend," he agreed.

"Legend?"

"I have never seen an Eldren try to handle the sword Kanajana."

"But you must assume that it is true. Otherwise…"

"Otherwise, there is little hope for Humanity." The words were dragged from his lips.

"Very well, Lord Katorn. You will assume that I am Erekosë, summoned by King Rigenos to lead Humanity to victory."

"I have no choice but to assume that."

"Good. And there is something that I, too, must assume, for my part, Lord Katorn."

"You? What?"

"I must assume that you will work *with* me in this enterprise. That there will be no plots behind my back, that there will be no information withheld from me that might prove vital, that you will not seek to make allies against me within our own ranks. You see, Lord Katorn, it could be your suspicions that might wreck our plans. A man jealous and resentful of his leader is capable of doing more harm than any enemy."

He nodded his head and straightened his shoulders, the hand falling away from his sword. "I had considered that question, my lord. I am not a fool."

"I know you are not a fool, Lord Katorn. If you were a fool, I should not have bothered to have had this conversation."

His tongue bulged in his cheek as he mulled over this statement. Eventually he said: "And you are not a fool, Lord Erekosë."

"Thank you. I did not suspect that you judge me that."

"Hmph." He removed his helmet and ran his fingers through his thick hair. He was still thinking.

I waited for him to say something further, but then he replaced his helmet firmly on his head, dug his thumb into the side of his mouth and picked at a tooth with the nail. He withdrew the thumb and stared at it intently for a moment. Then he looked at the map and murmured, "Well, at least we have an understanding. With that, it will be easier to fight this stinking war."

I nodded. "Much easier, I think."

He sniffed.

"How good is our own fleet?" I asked him.

"It's a fine fleet still. Not as large as it was, but we are remedying that, too. Our shipyards work night and day to build more and larger men-o'-war. And in our ironworks up and down the land we forge powerful guns with which to arm those ships."

"And what of men to crew them?"

"We are recruiting all we can. Even women are used in certain tasks—and boys. You were told that, Lord Erekosë, and it was true—the *whole* of Humanity fights the Eldren warriors."

I said nothing, but I had begun to admire the spirit of this people. I was less divided in my mind concerning the rights or wrongs of what I did. The folk of this strange time and place in which I found myself were fighting for nothing more nor less than the survival of their species.

But then another thought came to me. Could not the same be said of the Eldren?

I dismissed the thought.

At least Katorn and I had that in common. We refused to concern ourselves with speculation on moral and sentimental issues. We had a task to perform. We had assumed the responsibility for that task. We should do it to the best of our ability.

✺ 6 ✺

PREPARING FOR WAR

AND SO I talked with generals and with admirals. We pored over maps and discussed tactics, logistics, available men, animals and ships, while the fleets massed and the Two Continents were scoured for warriors, from boys of ten years old to men of fifty or older, from girls of twelve to women of sixty. All were marshalled beneath the double banner of Humanity which bore the arms of Zavara and Necralala and the standards of their king, Rigenos, and their war champion, Erekosë.

As the days passed, we planned the great land–sea invasion of Mernadin's chief harbour, Paphanaal, and the surrounding province, which was also called Paphanaal.

When not conferring with the commanders of the armies and navies, I practised weaponry, riding, until I became skilled in those arts.

It was not a question of *learning* so much as *remembering*. Just as the feel of my strange sword had been familiar, so was the sensation of a horse between my legs. Just as I had always known my name was Erekosë (which, I had been told, meant "The One Who Is Always There" in some ancient tongue of Humanity which was no longer used) so I had always known how to pull an arrow on a bowstring and let fly at a target as I galloped past on horseback.

But Iolinda—she was not familiar to me. Though there was some part of me that seemed able to travel through Time and Space and assume many incarnations, they were plainly not the same incarnations. I was not living an episode of my life over again, I had merely become the same person again, going through a different series of actions, or so it seemed. I had a sense of free will, within those terms. I did not feel that my fate was preordained. But perhaps it was. Perhaps I am too much of an optimist. Perhaps I am, after all, a fool and Katorn was wrong in his assessment of me. The Eternal Fool.

Certainly I was willing to make a fool of myself where Iolinda was concerned. Her beauty was almost unbearable. But with her I could not be a fool. She wanted a hero, an Immortal—and nothing less. So I must play the hero for her, to comfort her, though it went ill with my preferred manner, which has always been pretty casual. Sometimes, in fact, I felt more like her father than her would-be lover and, with my pat twentieth-century notions of human motivation, wondered if I were really nothing more than a substitute for the strong father she expected in Rigenos.

I think that she secretly despised Rigenos for not being more heroic, but I sympathised with the older man (older? I think it is I who am older, infinitely older—but enough of that) for Rigenos bore a great responsibility and bore it pretty well as far as I could make out. After all, he was a man who would rather plan pleasant gardens than battles. It was not his fault that he had been born a king without a close male successor to whom he could have, if he had been luckier, transferred responsibility. And I had heard that he bore himself well in battle and never backed away from any responsibility. King Rigenos was meant for a gentler life, maybe—though he could be fierce enough when it came to hating the Eldren. I was to be the hero that he felt incapable of being. I accepted that. But I was much more reluctant to be the father that he could not be. I wanted to enjoy a much healthier relationship with Iolinda or, so I told myself, I would not enjoy one at all!

I am not sure I had a choice. I was mesmerised by her. I would probably have accepted her on any terms.

We spent whatever time we could together, whenever I could get away from the military men and my own martial training. We would wander arm in arm along the closed balconies which covered the Palace of Ten Thousand Windows like a creeping plant, winding from top to bottom of the great palace and containing a superb variety of flowers, shrubs and caged and uncaged birds that fluttered through the foliage of these spiralling passages and perched amongst the branches of the vines and the small trees and sang to us as we wandered. I learned that this, too, had been King Rigenos's idea, to make the balconies more pleasant.

But that had been before the coming of the Eldren.

Slowly the day approached when the fleet would gather together and sail for the distant continent where the Eldren ruled. I had begun by being impatient to get to grips with the Eldren, but now I was becoming more and more reluctant to leave—for it would mean leaving Iolinda and my lust for her was growing quite as strongly as my love.

Although I gathered that day by day the society of humankind was becoming less and less open, more and more bound by unpleasant and unnecessary restrictions, it was still not considered wrong for unwed lovers to sleep together, so long as they were of an equal social standing. I was much relieved when

I discovered this. It seemed to me that an Immortal—as I was assumed to be—and a princess were quite decently matched. But it was not the social conventions that hampered my ambition— it was Iolinda herself. And that is one thing that no amount of freedom or "licence" or "permissiveness" or whatever the old fogies call it can cope with. That is the odd assumption found in the twentieth century (I wonder if you who read this will know what those two stupid words mean?): that if the laws that man makes concerning "morality"—particularly sexual morality— are done away with, then one huge orgy will begin. It forgets that people are, generally speaking, only attracted to a few other people and only fall in love with one or two in their whole lives. And there may be many other reasons why they may not be able to make love, even if their love is confirmed.

Where Iolinda was concerned, I hesitated because, as I have said, I did not wish to be merely a substitute for her father— and she hesitated because she needed to be absolutely sure she could "trust" me. John Daker would have called this a neurotic attitude. Perhaps it was, but on the other hand, was it neurotic for a relatively normal girl to feel a bit peculiar about someone she had only lately seen materialise from thin air?

But enough of this. All I should say is that, although we were both deeply in love at this point, we did not sleep together—we did not even discuss the matter, though it was often on the tip of my tongue.

What, in fact, began to happen was, oddly, that my lust began to wane. My love for Iolinda remained as strong as ever—if not stronger—but I did not feel any great need to express it in physical terms. It was not like me. Or perhaps I should say that it was not like John Daker!

However, as the day of departure came closer, I began to feel a need to express my love in some way and, one evening as we wandered through the balconies, I paused and put my hand under her hair and stroked the back of her neck and gently turned her to face me.

She looked sweetly up at me and smiled. Her red lips parted slightly and she did not move her head as I bent my own lips to hers and kissed her softly. My heart leaped. I held her close against me, feeling her breasts rise and fall against my chest. I lifted her hand and held it against my face as I looked down at her beauty. I thrust my hand deep into her hair and tasted her warm, sweet breath as we kissed again. She curled her fingers in mine and opened her eyes and her eyes were happy—truly happy for the first time. We drew apart.

Her breathing was now much less regular and she began to murmur something, but I cut her off short. She smiled at me expectantly, with a mixture of pride and tenderness.

"When I return," I said softly, "we shall be married."

She looked surprised for a moment and then she realised what I had said—the significance of what I had said. I was trying to tell her that she could trust me. It was the only way I could think of to do it. Perhaps a John Daker reflex, I don't know.

She nodded her head, drawing off her hand a wonderfully worked ring of gold, pearls and rose-coloured diamonds. This she placed on my little finger.

"A token of my love," she said. "An acceptance of your proposal. A charm, perhaps, to bring you luck in your battles. Something to remind you of me when you are tempted by those unhuman Eldren beauties." She smiled when she made this last retort.

"It has many functions," I said, "this ring."

"As many as you wish," she replied.

"Thank you."

"I love you, Erekosë," she said simply.

"I love you, Iolinda." I paused, then added, "But I am a

crude sort of lover, am I not? I have no token to give you. I feel embarrassed and a bit inadequate."

"Your word is enough," she said. "Swear that you will return to me."

I looked at her nonplussed for a second. Naturally I would return to her.

"Swear it," she said.

"I'll swear it. There is no question."

"Swear it again."

"I'll swear it a thousand times if once is not enough. I swear it. I swear that I will return to you, Iolinda, my love, my delight."

"Good." She seemed satisfied.

There came the sound of hurried footsteps along the balcony and we saw a slave I recognised as one of my own rushing towards us.

"Ah, master, there you are. King Rigenos has asked me to bring you to him."

It was late. "And what does King Rigenos want?" I asked.

"He did not say, master."

I smiled down at Iolinda and tucked her arm in mine. "Very well. We shall come."

~ 7 ~

THE ARMOUR OF EREKOSË

THE SLAVE LED us to my own apartments. They were empty of anyone save my retinue.

"But where is King Rigenos?" I asked.

"He said to wait here, master."

I smiled at Iolinda again. She smiled back. "Very well," I said. "We shall wait."

We did not wait long. Presently slaves began to arrive at my apartments. They were carrying bulky pieces of metal wrapped in oiled parchment and they began to pile it in the weapons room. I watched them with as little expression as possible, though I was greatly puzzled.

Then at last King Rigenos entered. He seemed much more excited than usual and Katorn was not, this time, with him.

"Greetings, Father," said Iolinda. "I…"

But King Rigenos raised a hand and turned to address the slaves. "Strip off the coverings," he said. "Hurry."

"King Rigenos," I said. "I would like to tell you that…"

"Forgive me, Lord Erekosë. First, look at what I have brought. It has lain for centuries in the vaults of the palace. Waiting, Erekosë—waiting for you!"

"Waiting?"

Then the oiled parchment was torn away and lay in curling heaps on the flagstones, revealing what was to me a magnificent sight.

"This," said the king, "is the armour of Erekosë. Broken from its tomb of rock deep beneath the palace's lowest dungeons so that Erekosë can wear it again."

The armour was black and it shone. It was as if it had been forged that day and forged by the greatest smith in history, for it was of exquisite workmanship.

I picked up the breastplate and ran my hand over it.

Unlike the armour worn by the Imperial Guard, this was smooth, without any kind of raised embellishment. The shoulder pieces were grooved, fanning high and away from the head, to channel a blow of sword, axe or lance from the wearer. The helmet, breastplate, greaves and the rest were all grooved in the same manner.

The metal was light, but very strong, like that of the sword. But the black lacquer shone. It shone brightly—almost blindingly. In its simplicity, the armour *was* beautiful—as beautiful as only really fine craftsmanship can be. Its sole ornament was a thick plume of scarlet horsehair which sprang from the crest of the helmet and cascaded down the smooth sides. I touched the armour with the reverence one has for fine art. In this case it was fine art designed to protect my life and my reverence was, if anything, that much greater!

"Thank you, King Rigenos," I said, and I was honestly grateful. "I will wear it on the day we set sail against the Eldren."

"That day is tomorrow," said King Rigenos quietly.

"What?"

"The last of our ships has come in. The last member of the crew is on board. The last cannon has been fitted. It will be a good tide tomorrow and we cannot miss it."

I glanced at him. Had I been misled in some way? Had Katorn prevailed upon the king not to let me know the exact time of sailing? But the king's expression showed no sign of a plot. I dismissed the idea and accepted what he said. I turned my gaze to Iolinda. She looked stricken.

"Tomorrow," she said.

"Tomorrow," confirmed King Rigenos.

I bit my lower lip. "Then I must prepare."

She said: "Father…"

He looked at her. "Yes, Iolinda?"

I began to speak and then paused. She glanced at me and was also silent. There was no easy way of telling him and suddenly it was as if we should keep our love, our pact, a secret. Neither of us knew why.

Tactfully the king withdrew. "I will discuss last-minute matters with you later, Lord Erekosë."

I bowed. He left.

Somewhat stunned, Iolinda and I stared at each other and then we moved into each other's arms and we wept.

John Daker would not have written this. He would have laughed at the sentiments, just as he would have scoffed at anyone who considered the arts of war important. John Daker would not have written this, but I must:

I began to feel a rising sense of excitement for the coming war. The old exultant mood started to sweep through me again. Overlaying my excitement was my love for Iolinda. This love seemed to be a calmer, purer love, so much more satisfying than casual, carnal love. It was a thing apart. Perhaps this was the chivalrous love which the peers of Christendom are said to have held above all other.

John Daker would have spoken of sexual repression and of swordplay as a substitute for sexual intercourse.

Perhaps John Daker would have been right. But it did not seem to me that he was right, though I was well aware of all the rationalist arguments that supported such a view. There is a great tendency for the human race to see all other times in its own terms. The terms of this society were subtly different—I was only dimly aware of many of the differences. I was responding to Iolinda in those terms. It is all I can say. And later events, I suppose, were also played out in those terms.

I took Iolinda's face in my two hands and I bent and I kissed her forehead and she kissed my lips and then she left.

"Shall I see you before I leave?" I asked as she reached the door.

"Yes," she said. "Yes, my love, if it is possible."

When she had gone, I did not feel sad. I inspected the armour once again and then I went down to the main hall, where King Rigenos stood with many of his greatest captains, studying a large map of Mernadin and the waters between it and Necralala.

"We start here in the morning," Rigenos told me, indicating the harbour area of Necranal. The River Droonaa flowed through Necranal to the sea and the port of Noonos, where the fleet was assembled. "There must be a certain amount of ceremony, I fear, Erekosë. Various rituals to perform. I have already sketched them to you, I believe."

"You have," I said. "The ceremony seems more arduous than the warfare."

The captains laughed. Though somewhat distant and a trifle wary of me, they liked me well enough, for I had proved (to my own astonishment) to have a natural grasp of tactics and the warlike arts.

"But the ceremony is necessary," Rigenos said, "for the people. It makes a reality for them, you see. They can experience something of what we shall be doing."

"We?" I said. "Am I wrong? I thought you implied that you were sailing, too."

"l am," Rigenos said quietly. "I decided that it was necessary."

"Necessary?"

"Yes." He would say no more, particularly in front of his marshals. "Now, let us continue. We must all of us rise very early tomorrow morning."

As we discussed these final matters of order and tactics and logistics, I studied the king's face as best I could.

No one expected him to sail with his armies. He would lose no face at all by remaining behind in his capital. Yet he had made a decision which would put him in a position of extreme danger and cause him to take actions for which he had no palate.

Why had he made the decision? To prove to himself that he could fight, perhaps? Yet he had proved it already. Because he was jealous of me? Because he did not altogether trust me? I glanced at Katorn, but saw nothing in Katorn's face to indicate satisfaction. Katorn was merely his usual surly self.

Mentally I shrugged. Speculation at this point would get me nowhere. The fact was that the king, not an altogether robust man now, was coming with us. It might give extra inspiration to our warriors, at least. It might also help control Katorn's particular tendencies.

Eventually we dispersed and went our ways. I went straight to my bed and, before I slept, lay there peacefully, thinking of Iolinda, thinking of the battle plans I had helped hatch, wondering what the Eldren would be like to fight—I still had no completely clear idea of how they fought (save "treacherously and ferociously") or even what they looked like (save that they resembled "demons from the deepest pits").

I knew I would soon have some of the answers, at any rate. Soon I was asleep.

* * *

My dreams were strange dreams on that night before we sailed for Mernadin.

I saw towers and marshes and lakes and armies and lances that shot flames and metallic flying machines whose wings flapped like those of gigantic birds. I saw monstrously large flamingoes, strange masklike helmets resembling the faces of beasts.

I saw dragons—huge reptiles with fiery venom, flapping across dark, moody skies. I saw a beautiful city tumbling in flames. I saw unhuman creatures that I knew to be gods. I saw a woman whom I could not name, a small red-headed man who seemed to be my friend. A sword—a great, black sword more powerful than the one I now owned—a sword that perhaps, oddly, was myself!

I saw a world of ice across which strange, great ships with billowing sails ran and black beasts like whales propelled themselves over endless plateaux of white.

I saw a world—or was it a universe?—that had no horizon and was filled with a rich, jewelled mosaic atmosphere which changed all the time and from which people and objects emerged only to disappear again. It was somewhere beyond the Earth, I was sure. Yes—I was aboard a spaceship—but a ship that travelled through no universe conceived of by Man.

I saw a desert through which I stumbled weeping and I was alone—lonelier than any man had ever been.

I saw a jungle—a jungle of primitive trees and gigantic ferns. And through the ferns I saw huge, bizarre buildings and there was a weapon in my hand that was not a sword and was not a gun, but it was more powerful than either.

I rode strange beasts and encountered stranger people. I moved through landscapes that were beautiful and terrifying. I piloted flying machines and spaceships and I drove chariots. I hated. I fell in love. I built empires and caused the collapse of nations and I slew many and was slain many times. I triumphed and was humiliated. And I had many names. The names roared in my skull. Too many names. Too many...

And there was no peace. There was only strife.

8

THE SAILING

NEXT MORNING I awoke and my dreams went away and I was left in an introspective mood and there was only one thing that I desired.

That thing was an Upmann's Coronas Major.

I kept trying to push the name from my mind. To my knowledge John Daker had never smoked an Upmann's. He would not have known one cigar from another! Where had the name come from? Another name came into my head—Jeremiah. And that, too, was vaguely familiar.

I sat up in bed and I recognised my surroundings and the two names merged with the other names I had dreamed of and I got up and entered the next chamber where slaves were finishing preparing my bath. With relief I got into the bath and, as I washed my body, I began to concentrate once again on the problem at hand. Yet a sense of depression remained with me and again for a moment I wondered if I were mad and involved in some complicated schizophrenic fantasy.

When the slaves brought in my armour I began to feel much better. Again I marvelled at its beauty and its craftsmanship.

And now the time had come to put it on. First I donned my

underclothes, then a sort of quilted overall and then I began to strap the armour about me. Again it was easy to find the appropriate straps and buckles. It was as if I had clad myself in this armour every morning of my life. It fitted perfectly. It was comfortable and no weight at all, though it completely covered my body.

Next, I strode to the weapons room and took down the great sword that hung there and I drew the belt of metal links around my waist and settled the poisonous sword in its protecting scabbard against my left hip, tossed back the scarlet plume on my helmet, lifted the visor and was ready.

Slaves escorted me down to the Great Hall, where the peers of Humanity had assembled to make their final leave-taking with Necranal.

The tapestries which had earlier hung on the walls of beaten silver had now been removed and in their place were hundreds of bright banners. These were the banners of the marshals, the captains and the knights, who were gathered there in splendid array, assembled according to rank.

On a specially erected dais the throne of the king had been placed. The dais was hung with a cloth of emerald green and behind it were the twin banners of the Two Continents. I took my place before the dais and we waited tensely for the arrival of the king. I had already been coached concerning the responses I was to make in the forthcoming ceremony.

At last there came a great yelling of trumpets and beating of martial drums from the gallery above us and through a door came the king.

King Rigenos had gained stature, it seemed, for he wore a suit of gilded armour over which was hung a surcoat of white and red. Set into his helmet was his crown of iron and diamonds. He walked proudly to the dais and ascended it, seating himself in his throne with both arms stretched along the arms of the seat.

We raised our hands in salute:

"Hail, King Rigenos!" we roared.

And then we kneeled. I kneeled first. Behind me kneeled the little group of marshals. Behind them were a hundred captains, behind them were five thousand knights, all kneeling. And surrounding us, along the walls, were the old nobles, the ladies of the court, men-at-arms at attention, slaves and squires, the mayors of the various quarters of the city and from the various provinces of the Two Continents.

And all watched Rigenos and his champion, Erekosë.

King Rigenos rose from his throne. I looked up at him and his face was grave and stern. I had never before seen him look so much a king.

Now I felt that the attention of the watchers was on myself alone. I, Erekosë, Champion of Humanity, was to be their saviour. They knew it.

In my confidence and pride, I knew it, also.

King Rigenos raised his hands and spread them out and began to speak:

"Erekosë the Champion, Marshals, Captains and Knights of Humanity—we go to wage war against unhuman evil. We go to fight something that is more than an enemy bent on conquest. We go to fight a menace that would destroy our entire race. We go to save our two fair continents from total annihilation. The victor will rule the entire Earth. The defeated will become dust and will be forgotten—it will be as if he had never existed.

"This expedition upon which we are about to embark will be decisive. With Erekosë to lead us, we shall win the port of Paphanaal and its surrounding province. But that will only be the first stage in our campaigns."

King Rigenos paused and then spoke again into the almost

absolute silence that had fallen in the Great Hall.

"More battle must follow fast upon the first so that the hated Hounds of Evil will, once and for all, be destroyed. Men and women—even children—must perish. We drove them to their holes in the Mountains of Sorrow once, but this time we must not let their race survive. Let only their memory remain for a little while—to remind us what evil is!"

Still kneeling, I raised both my hands above my head and clenched my fists.

"Erekosë," said King Rigenos. "You who by the power of your eternal will made yourself into flesh again and came to us at this time of need, you will be the power with which we shall destroy the Eldren. You will be Humanity's scythe to sweep this way and that and cut the Eldren down as weeds. You will be Humanity's spade to dig up the roots wherever they have grown. You will be Humanity's fire to burn the waste to the finest ash. You, Erekosë, will be the wind that will blow those ashes away as if they had never existed! You will destroy the Eldren!"

"*I will destroy the Eldren!*" I cried and my voice echoed through the Great Hall like the voice of a god. "*I will destroy the enemies of Humanity! With the sword Kanajana I will ride upon them with vengeance and hatred and cruelty in my heart and I will vanquish the Eldren!*"

From behind me now came a mighty shout:

"*WE SHALL VANQUISH THE ELDREN!*"

Now the king raised his head and his eyes glittered and his mouth was hard.

"Swear it!" he said.

We were intoxicated by the atmosphere of hate and rage in the Great Hall.

"*We so swear!*" we roared. "*We will destroy the Eldren!*"

Hatred seared from the king's eyes, trembled in his voice:

"Go now, Paladins of Mankind. Go—*destroy the Eldren offal. Clean our planet of the Eldren filth!*"

As one man, we rose to our feet and yelled our battle-cries, turned in precision and marched from the Great Hall, out of the Palace of Ten Thousand Windows and into a day noisy with the swelling cheers of the people.

But as we marched, one thought preyed on my mind. Where was Iolinda? Why had she not come to me? There had been so little time before the ceremony and yet I would have thought she would have sent a message at least.

Down the winding streets of Necranal we marched in glorious procession. Through the cheering day with the bright sun shining on our weapons and our armour and our flags of a thousand rich colours waving in the wind.

And I led them. I, Erekosë, the Eternal, the Champion, the Vengeance Bringer—I led them. My arms were raised as if I were already celebrating my victory. Pride filled me. I knew what glory was and I relished it. This was the way to live—as a warrior, a leader of great armies, a wielder of weapons.

On we marched, down towards the waiting ships which were ready on the river. And a song came to my lips—a song that was in an archaic version of the language I now spoke. I sang the song and it was taken up by all the warriors who marched behind me. Drums began to beat and trumpets to shout, and we cried aloud for blood and death and the great red reaping that would come to Mernadin.

That is how we marched. That is how we felt.

Do not judge me until I have told you more.

We reached the wide part of the river where the harbour was and there were the ships. There were fifty ships stretched along both quays on either side of the river. Fifty ships bearing the fifty standards of fifty proud paladins.

And these were only fifty. The fleet itself waited for us to join it at the port of Noonos. Noonos of the Jewelled Towers.

The people of Necranal lined the banks of the river. They were cheering, cheering—so that we became used to their voices as men become used to the sounds of the sea, scarcely hearing them.

I regarded the ships. Richly decorated cabins were built on the decks and the ships of the paladins had several masts bearing furled sails of painted canvas. Already oars were being slipped through the ports and dipped into the placid river waters. Strong men, three to a sweep, sat upon the rowing benches. These men were not, as far as I could see, slaves, but free warriors.

At the head of this squadron of ships lay the king's huge battle-barge—a magnificent man-o'-war. It had eighty pairs of oars and eight tall masts. Its rails were painted in red, gold and black, its decks were polished crimson, its sails were yellow, dark blue and orange and its huge carved figurehead, representing a goddess holding a sword in her two outstretched hands, was predominantly scarlet and silver. Ornate and splendid, the deck cabins shone with fresh varnish which had been laid over pictures of ancient human heroes (I was among them, though the likenesses were poor) and ancient human victories, of mythical beasts and demons and gods.

Detaching myself from the main force that had drawn itself up on the quayside, I walked to the tapestry-covered gangway and strode up it and boarded the ship. Sailors rushed forward to greet me.

One said: "The Princess Iolinda awaits you in the Grand Cabin, excellency."

I turned and then paused, looking at the splendid structure of the cabin, smiling slightly at the representations of myself painted upon it. Then I moved towards it and entered a comparatively low door into a room which was covered, floor, walls and ceiling, with thick tapestries in deep reds and blacks and golds. Lanterns hung in the room, and in the shadows, clad in a simple dress and a thin, dark cloak, stood my Iolinda.

"I did not wish to interrupt the preparations this morning," she said. "My father said that they were important—that there was little time to spare. So I thought you would not want to see me."

I smiled. "You still do not believe what I say, do you, Iolinda? You still do not trust me when I proclaim my love for you, when I tell you that I would do anything for you." I went towards her and held her in my arms. "I love you, Iolinda. I shall always love you."

"And I shall always love you, Erekosë. You will live for ever, but…"

"There is no proof of that," I said gently. "And I am by no means invulnerable, Iolinda. I sustained enough cuts and bruises in my weapons practice to realise that!"

"You will not die, Erekosë."

"I would be happier if I shared your conviction!"

"Do not laugh at me, Erekosë. I will not be patronised!"

"I am not laughing at you, Iolinda. I am not condescending to you. I only speak the truth. You must face that truth. You must."

"Very well," she said. "I will face it. But I feel that you will not die. Yet, I have such strange premonitions—I feel that something worse than death could befall us."

"Your fears are natural, but they are baseless. There is no need for gloom, my dear. Look at the fine armour I wear, the powerful sword I bear, the mighty force I command."

"Kiss me, Erekosë."

I kissed her. I kissed her for a long time and then she broke from my arms and ran to the door and was gone.

I stared at the door, half thinking of running after her, of reassuring her. But I knew that I could not reassure her. Her fears were not really rational—they reflected her constant sense of insecurity. I promised myself that later I would give her proof of security. I would bring constants into her life—things she could trust.

Trumpets sounded. King Rigenos was coming aboard.

A few moments later the king entered the cabin, tugging off his crowned helm. Katorn was behind him, as sullen as ever.

"The people seem enthusiastic," I said. "The ceremony seemed to have the effect you desired, King Rigenos."

Rigenos nodded wearily. "Aye." The ritual had plainly taken much from him and he slumped into a hanging chair in the corner and called for wine. "We'll be sailing soon. When, Katorn?"

"Within the quarter-hour, my lord king." Katorn took the jug of wine from the slave who brought it and poured Rigenos a cup without offering one to me.

King Rigenos waved his hand. "Would you have some wine, Lord Erekosë?"

I declined. "You spoke well in the hall, King Rigenos," I said. "You fired us with a fine bloodlust."

Katorn sniffed. "Let us hope it lasts until we get to the enemy," he said. "We have some raw soldiers sailing on this expedition. Half our warriors have never fought before—and half of those are boys. There are even women in some detachments, I've heard."

"You seem pessimistic, Lord Katorn," I said.

He grunted. "It is as well to be. This finery and grandeur is all right for cheering up the civilians, but it's best you don't believe it yourself. You should know, Erekosë. You should know what real war is all about—pain, fear, death. There's nothing else to it."

"You forget," I said. "My memory of my own past is clouded."

Katorn sniffed and gobbled down his wine. He replaced the cup with a clatter and left. "I'll see to the casting off."

The king cleared his throat. "You and Katorn…" he began, but broke off. "You…"

"We are not friends," I said. "I dislike his surly, mistrustful manner—and he suspects me of being a fraud, a traitor, a spy of some sort."

King Rigenos nodded. "He has hinted as much to me." He sipped his wine. "I told him that I saw you materialise with my own eyes, that there is no question you are Erekosë, that there is no reason not to trust you—but he persists. Why, do you think? He is a sane, sensible soldier."

"He is jealous," I said. "I have taken over his power."

"But he was as agreed as any of us that we needed a new leader who would inspire our people in the fight against the Eldren!"

"In principle, perhaps," I said. I shrugged. "It does not matter, King Rigenos. I think we have worked out a compromise."

King Rigenos was lost in his own thoughts. "There again," he murmured, "it could have nothing to do with war, at all."

"What do you mean?"

He gave me a candid look. "It might concern matters of love, Erekosë. Katorn has always been pleased by Iolinda's manner."

"You could be right. But again there is nothing I can do. Iolinda seems to prefer my company."

"Katorn might see it as mere infatuation with an ideal rather than a real person."

"Do you see it as that?"

"I do not know. I have not talked to Iolinda about it."

"Well," I said, "perhaps we shall see when we return."

"*If* we return," said King Rigenos. "In that, I must admit, I'm in agreement with Katorn. Overconfidence has often been the main cause of many defeats."

I nodded. "Perhaps you are right."

There came shouts and cries from outside and the ship lurched suddenly as the ropes were cast off and the anchors hauled in.

"Come," said King Rigenos. "Let us go out on deck. It will be expected of us." Hastily he finished his wine and placed his crowned helmet upon his head. We left the cabin together and, as we came out, the cheering on the quayside swelled louder and louder.

We stood there waving to the people as the drums began to pound out the slow rowing rhythm. I saw Iolinda seated in her carriage, her body half-turned to watch as we left. I waved to her and she raised her own arm in a final salute.

"Goodbye, Iolinda," I murmured.

Katorn darted me a cynical look from the corner of his eye as he passed to supervise the rowing.

Goodbye, Iolinda.

The wind had dropped. I was sweating in my war-gear, for the day was oppressed by a great flaming sun, blazing in a cloudless sky.

I continued to wave from the stern of the swaying vessel, keeping my gaze on Iolinda as she sat there erect in her carriage, and then we had rounded a bend in the river and saw only the rearing towers of Necranal above and behind us, heard only the distant cheering.

We beat down the Droonaa River, moving fast with the current towards Noonos of the Jewelled Towers—and the fleets.

9

AT NOONOS

OH THESE BLIND *and bloody wars...*

"Really, Bishop, you fail to understand that human affairs are resolved in terms of action."

Brittle arguments, pointless causes, cynicism disguised as pragmatism.

"Would you not rest, my son?"

"I cannot rest, Father, while the Paynim horde is already on the banks of the Danube."

"Peace..."

"Will they be content with peace?"

"Perhaps."

"They won't be satisfied with Vietnam. They won't be content until the whole of Asia is theirs... And after that, the world."

"We are not beasts."

"We must act as beasts. They act as beasts."

"But if we tried..."

"We have tried."

"Have we?"

"Fire must be fought with fire."

"Is there no other way?"

"There is no other way."

"The children..."

"There is no other way."

A gun. A sword. A bomb. A bow. A vibrapistol. A flame lance. An axe. A club.

"There is no other way."

On board the flagship that night, as the oars rose and fell and the drum continued its steady beat and the timbers creaked and the waves lapped at the hull, I slept poorly. Fragments of conversations. Phrases. Images. They tumbled in my tired brain and refused to leave me in peace. A thousand different periods of history. A million different faces. But the situation was always the same. The argument—made in myriad tongues—did not change.

Only when I rose from my bunk did my head clear and at length I resolved to go on deck.

What sort of creature was I? Why did it seem that I was for ever doomed to drift from era to era and act out the same rôle wherever I went? What trick—what cosmic joke had been played upon me?

The night air was cool on my face and the moonlight struck through the light clouds at regular intervals so that the beams looked like the spokes of some gigantic wheel. It was as if the chariot of a god had sunk through the low cloud and become embedded in the coarser air beneath.

I stared at the water and saw the clouds reflected in it, saw them break to reveal the moon. It was the same moon I had known as John Daker. The same bland face could be made out staring down in contentment at the antics of the creatures of the planet it circled. How many disasters had that moon witnessed? How many foolish crusades? How many wars and battles and murders?

The clouds moved together again and the waters of the river grew black as if to say that I would never find the revelation I sought.

I looked to the banks. We were passing through a thick forest. The tops of the trees were silhouetted against the slightly lighter darkness of the night. A few night animals voiced their cries from time to time and it seemed to me that they were lonely cries, lost cries, pitiful cries. I sighed and leaned against the rail and watched the water creamed grey by the slashing oars.

I had better accept that I must fight again. Again? Where had I fought before? What did my vague memories mean? What significance had my dreams? The simple answer—the pragmatic answer (or certainly one that John Daker could have best understood)—was that I was mad. My imagination was overwrought. Perhaps I had never been John Daker. Perhaps he, too, was another crazed invention.

I must fight again.

That was all there was to it. I had accepted the rôle and I must play it to the finish.

My brain began to clear as the moon set and dawn lightly touched the horizon.

I watched the sun rise, a huge scarlet disc moving with steady grandeur into the sky, as if curious to discover the sounds that disturbed the world—the beat of the drum, the crack of the oars.

"You are not sleeping, Lord Erekosë. You are eager, I see, to do battle."

I felt I did not need Katorn's banter added to the burden. "I thought I would enjoy watching the sun rise," I said.

"And the moon set?" Katorn's voice implied something that I could not quite grasp. "You seem to like the night, Lord Erekosë."

"Sometimes," I said. "It is peaceful," I added as significantly as I could. "There is little to disturb a man's thoughts in the night."

"True. You have something in common with our enemies, then."

I turned impatiently, regarding his dark features with anger. "What do you mean?"

"I meant only that the Eldren, too, are said to prefer the night to the day."

"If it is true of me, my lord," I said, "then it will be a great asset to us in our war with them if I can fight them by night as well as by day."

"I hope so, my lord."

"Why do you mistrust me so, Lord Katorn?"

He shrugged. "Did I say that I did? We struck a bargain, remember?"

"And I have kept my part of it."

"And I mine. I will follow you, do not doubt that. Whatever I suspect, I will still follow you."

"Then I would ask you to discontinue these little jibes of yours. They are naïve. They serve no purpose."

"They serve a purpose for me, Lord Erekosë. They ease my temper—they channel it into a suitable area."

"I have sworn my oath to Humanity," I told him. "I will serve King Rigenos's cause. I have my own burdens to bear, Lord Katorn."

"I am deeply sympathetic."

I turned away. I had come close to making a fool of myself— appealing to Katorn for mercy, almost, by claiming my own problems as an excuse.

"Thank you, Lord Katorn," I said coldly. The ship began to turn a bend in the river and I thought I could see the sea ahead. "I am grateful for your understanding." I slapped at my face. The ship was passing through a cloud of midges hovering over the river. "These insects are irritating, are they not?"

"Perhaps it would be best if you did not allow yourself to be subjected to their intentions, my lord," Katorn replied.

"Indeed, I think you are right, Lord Katorn. I will go below."

"Good morrow, my lord."

"Good morrow, Lord Katorn."

I left him standing on the deck and staring moodily ahead.

In other circumstances, I thought, *I would slay that man.*

As it was, there seemed a growing chance that he would do his utmost to slay me. I wondered if Rigenos were correct and Katorn was doubly jealous of me—jealous of my reputation as a warrior, jealous of Iolinda's love for me.

I washed and dressed myself in my war-gear and refused to bother myself with all these pointless thoughts. A little later I heard the helmsman shout and went on deck to see what his call signified.

Noonos was in sight. We all crowded the rails to get a glimpse of this fabulous city. We were half blinded by the glare from the towers for they were truly jewelled. The city flared with light—a great white aura speckled with a hundred other colours, green and violet and pink and mauve and ochre and red, all dancing in the brighter glow created by a million gems.

And beyond Noonos lay the sea—a calm sea gleaming in the sunshine.

As Noonos came closer, the river widened until it was clear that this was where it opened into the ocean. The banks became more and more distant and we kept closer to the starboard bank, for that was the bank on which Noonos was built. There were other towns and villages dotted amongst the wooded hills overlooking the river mouth. Some of them were picturesque, but they were all dominated by the port we were approaching.

Now seabirds began to squeal around our topmast and, with a great flapping of wings, settle in the yards and squabble, it appeared, for the best spot in the rigging.

The rhythm of the oars became slower and we began to back water as we approached the harbour itself. Behind us the squadron of proud ships dropped anchor. They would join us later when the pilot had come out to give them their mooring order.

Leaving our sister ships behind, we rowed slowly into Noonos, flying the standard of King Rigenos and the standard of Erekosë—a black field supporting a silver sword.

And the cheering began again. Held back by soldiers in armour of quilted leather, the crowds craned their necks to see us as we disembarked. And then, as I walked down the gangplank and appeared on the quayside, a huge chanting began that startled me at first when I realised what the word was that they were chanting.

"*EREKOSË! EREKOSË! EREKOSË! EREKOSË!*"

I raised my right arm in salute and almost staggered as the noise increased until it was literally deafening. I could barely refrain from covering my ears!

Prince Bladagh, Overlord of Noonos, greeted us with due ceremony and read out a speech that could not be heard for the shouting, and then we were escorted through the streets towards the quarters we were to use while making our brief stay in the city.

The jewelled towers were not disappointing, though I noticed that the houses built closer to the ground made a great contrast. Many of them were little better than hovels. It was quite plain where the money came from to encrust the towers with rubies, pearls and emeralds.

I had not noticed this great disparity between the rich and the poor in Necranal. Either I had been too impressed by the newness of the sights or the royal city took pains to disguise any areas of poverty, if they indeed existed.

And there were ragged people here, to go with the hovels, though they cheered as loudly as the rest, if not louder. Perhaps they blamed the Eldren for their misery.

Prince Bladagh was a sallow-featured man of about forty-five. He had a long, drooping moustache, pale, watery eyes and his gestures were those of an irritable but fastidious vulture. It emerged, and I was not surprised, that he would not be joining us in our expedition but would remain behind "to protect the city"—or his own gold most likely, I thought.

"Ah, now, my liege," he muttered as we reached his palace and the jewelled gates swung back to admit us (I noticed that they would have shone better if they had been cleaned). "Ah, now—my palace is yours, King Rigenos. And yours, too, Lord Erekosë, of course. Anything you need."

"A hot meal—and a simple one," King Rigenos said, echoing my own sentiments. "No banquets. I warned you not to make a large ceremony of this, Bladagh."

"And I have not, my liege." Bladagh looked relieved. He did not seem to me to be a man who enjoyed spending money. "I have not."

The meal *was* simple, though not particularly well-prepared. We ate it with Prince Bladagh, his plump, stupid wife, Princess Ionante, and their two scrawny children. Privately I was amused at the contrast between the city seen from a distance and the appearance and way of life of its ruler.

A short while later the various commanders who had been assembling in Noonos for the past several weeks arrived to confer with Rigenos and myself. Katorn was among them and was able to outline very succinctly and graphically the battle plans we had worked out between us in Necranal.

Among the commanders were several famous heroes of the Two Continents—Count Roldero, a burly aristocrat whose armour was as workmanlike and free from decoration as my own; also there was Prince Malihar and his brother, Duke Ezak, both of whom had been through many campaigns; Earl Shanura of Karakoa, one of the farthest provinces and one of the most barbaric. Shanura wore his hair long, in three plaits that hung down his back. His pale features were gaunt and criss-crossed with scars. He spoke seldom and usually to ask specific questions. The variety of the faces and the costumes surprised me at first. At least, I thought ironically, Humanity was united on this world, which was more than could be said for the world John Daker had left. But perhaps they were only united for the moment, to defeat the common enemy. After that, I thought, their unity might well suffer a setback. Earl Shanura, for instance, did not seem too happy about taking orders from King Rigenos, whom he probably considered soft.

I hoped that I could keep so disparate a group of officers together in the battles that were to follow.

At last we were finished with our discussions and I had spoken a word or two with every commander there. King Rigenos glanced at the bronze clock that stood on the table and which was marked with sixteen divisions. "It will be time to put to sea soon," he said. "Are all ships ready?"

"Mine have been ready for months," Earl Shanura said gruffly. "I was beginning to feel they would rot before they saw action."

The others agreed that their ships would be able to sail with little more than an hour's notice.

Rigenos and I thanked Bladagh and his family for their hospitality and they seemed rather more cheerful now that we were leaving.

Instead of marching from the palace, we now hurried in coaches to the quayside and rapidly boarded our ships. The king's flagship was called the *Iolinda*, a fact which I had not noticed before, my thoughts being full of the woman who bore that name. Our other ships from Necranal were now in port and their sailors were refreshing themselves in the short time they had, while slaves took on board the last provisions and armaments that were needed.

There was still a mood of slight depression hanging over me from my strange half-dreams of the previous night, but it was beginning to disperse as my excitement grew. It was still a month's sailing to Mernadin, but already I was beginning to relish the chance of action. At least action would help me forget the other problems. I was reminded of something that Pierre told Andrei in *War and Peace*—something about all men finding their own ways of forgetting the fact of death. Some womanised, some gambled, some drank and some, paradoxically, made war. Well, it was not the fact of death that obsessed me—indeed, it seemed that it was the fact of eternal existence that was preying on my mind. An eternal life involving eternal warfare.

Would I at some stage discover the truth? I was not sure that I wanted to know the truth. The thought frightened me. Perhaps a god could have accepted it. But I was not a god. I was a man. I knew I was a man. My problems, my ambitions, my emotions were on a human scale, save for the one abiding problem—the question of how I came to exist in this form, of how I had become what I was. Or was I truly eternal? Was there no beginning and no end to my existence? The very nature of Time was held in question. I could no longer regard Time as being linear, as I had once done as John Daker. Time could not be conceived of any longer in spacial terms.

I needed a philosopher, a magician, a scientist to help me on that problem. Or else I could forget it. But could I forget it? I would have to try.

The seabirds squawked and circled as the sails smacked down and swelled in the sultry wind that had started to blow. The timbers creaked as the anchors were weighed and the mooring ropes cast off from the capstans and the great flagship, *Iolinda*, heaved herself from the port, her oars still rising and falling, but making faster speed now as she sailed towards the open sea.

~ 10 ~

FIRST SIGHT OF THE ELDREN

THE FLEET WAS huge and contained great fighting ships of many kinds, some resembling what John Daker would have called nineteenth-century tea clippers, some that looked like junks, some with the lateen rig of Mediterranean craft, some that were very like Elizabethan caravels. Sailing in their separate formations, according to their province of origin, they symbolised the differences and the unity of mankind. I was proud of them.

Excited, tense, alert and confident of victory, we sailed for Paphanaal, gateway to Mernadin and conquest.

Yet I still felt the need to know more of the Eldren. My cloudy memory of the life of an earlier Erekosë could only conjure an impression of confused battles against them and also, perhaps, somewhere a feeling of emotional pain. That was all. I had heard that they had no orbs to their eyes and that this was their chief distinguishing non-human characteristic. They were said to be inhumanly beautiful, inhumanly merciless, and with inhuman sexual appetites. They were slightly taller than the average man, had long heads with high cheekbones and slightly slanting eyes. But this was not really enough for me. There were no pictures of Eldren anywhere on the Two Continents. Pictures were supposed to bring bad luck, particularly if the evil eyes of the Eldren were depicted.

As we sailed, there was a great deal of ship-to-ship communication, with commanders being rowed or hauled in slings to and from the flagship, depending on the weather. We had worked out our basic strategy and had contingency plans in case it should prove impossible to exercise. The idea had been mine and seemed a new one to the others, but they soon grasped it and the details had now all been decided upon. Each day the warriors of every ship were drilled in what they were to do when the Eldren fleet was sighted, if it was sighted. If it was not, we should dispatch part of the fleet straight to Paphanaal and begin the attack on the city. However, we expected the Eldren to send out their defence fleet to meet us before we reached Paphanaal and it was on this probability that we based our main plan.

Katorn and I avoided each other as much as possible. There were, in those first few days of sailing, none of the verbal duels of the sort we had had in Necranal and on the Droonaa River. I was polite to Katorn when we had need to communicate and he, in his surly way, was polite to me. King Rigenos seemed to be relieved and told me that he was glad we had settled our differences. We had not, of course, settled anything. We had merely waived those differences until such time as we could decide them once and for all. I knew eventually that I must fight Katorn or that he would try to murder me.

I took a liking to Count Roldero of Stalaco, though he was perhaps the most bloodthirsty of all when it came to discussing the Eldren. John Daker would have called him a reactionary, but he would have liked him. He was a staunch, stoical, honest man who spoke his mind and allowed others to speak theirs, expecting the same tolerance from them as he gave. When I had once suggested to him that he saw things too plainly in black and white, he smiled wearily and replied:

"Erekosë, my friend, when you have seen what I have of the events that have taken place in my lifetime on this planet of ours, then you will see things quite as clearly in black and white as I do. You can only judge people by their actions, not by their protestations. People act for good or they act for ill and those who do great ill are bad and those who do great good—they are good."

"But people may do great good accidentally, though with evil intentions—and conversely people may do great evil though having the best of intentions," I said, amused by his assumption that he had lived longer and seen more than I had—though I think his assumption was meant in jest.

"Exactly!" Count Roldero replied. "You have only repeated my point. I do not care, as I said, what people protest their intentions to be. I judge them by the results they achieve. Take the Eldren…"

I raised my hand, laughing. "I know how wicked they are. Everyone has told me of their cunning, their treachery, their black powers."

"Ah, you seem to think I hate Eldren individuals. I do not. For all I know they may be kind to their own children, love their wives and treat their animals well. I do not say that they are, as individuals, monsters. It is as a force that they must be considered. It is what they do that must be judged. It is on the threat of their own ambitions that we must base our attitude towards them."

"And how do you consider that force?" I asked.

"It is not human, therefore its interests are not human. Therefore, in terms of its own self-interest, it needs to destroy us. In this case, because the Eldren are not human, they threaten us merely by existing. And, by the same token, we threaten them.

They understand this and would wipe us out. We understand this and would wipe them out before they have the chance to destroy us. You understand?"

The argument seemed convincing enough to the pragmatist that I considered myself to be. But a thought came to mind and I voiced it.

"Are you not forgetting one thing, Count Roldero? You have said it yourself—the Eldren are *not* human. You are assuming that they have human interests."

"They are flesh and blood," he said. "They are beasts, as we are beasts. They have those impulses, just as we have them."

"But many species of beast seem to live together in basic harmony," I reminded him. "The lion does not constantly war with the leopard; the horse does not war with the cow; even among themselves they rarely kill each other, no matter how important the issue to them."

"But they would," said Count Roldero, undaunted. "They would if they could anticipate events. They would if they could work out the rate at which the rival animal is consuming food, breeding, expanding its territory."

I gave up. I felt we were both on shaky ground now. We were seated in my cabin, looking out at a beautiful evening and a calm sea through the open porthole. I poured Count Roldero more wine from my dwindling store (I had taken to drinking a good deal of wine shortly before I went to bed, to insure myself of a rest not broken by visions and memories).

Count Roldero quaffed the wine and stood up. "It's getting late. I must return to my ship or my men will think I've drowned and be celebrating. I see you're running short of wine. I'll bring a skin or two on my next visit. Farewell, friend Erekosë. Your heart's in the right place, I'm sure. But you're a sentimentalist, for all you say to the contrary."

I grinned. "Goodnight, Roldero." I raised my half-full wine-cup. "Let's drink to peace when this business is over!"

Roldero snorted. "Aye, peace—like the cows and the horses! Goodnight, my friend." He left laughing.

Rather drunkenly, I removed my clothes and fell into my bunk, chuckling foolishly at Roldero's parting remark. "Like the cows and the horses. He's right. Who wants to lead a life like that? Here's to war!" And I flung the wine-cup through the open porthole and fell to snoring almost before my eyes had closed.

And I dreamed.

But this time I dreamed of the wine-cup I had hurled through the porthole. I imagined I saw it bobbing on the waves, its gold and jewels glittering. I imagined I saw it caught by a current and borne far away from the fleet—out to a lonely place where ships never sailed and land was never in sight, tossed for ever on a bleak sea.

For the whole month of our sailing, the sea was calm, the wind good and the weather, on the whole, fine.

Our spirits rose higher. We took this to be a sign of good luck. All of us were cheerful. All, that is, save Katorn, who grumbled that this could well be the calm before the storm, that we must expect the worst of the Eldren when we eventually engaged.

"They are tricky," he would say. "Those filth are tricky. Even now they could know of our coming and have planned some manoeuvre we are not expecting. They might even be responsible for the weather."

I could not help laughing openly at this and he stalked off up the deck in anger. "You will see, Lord Erekosë," he called back. "You will see!"

And the next day the opportunity came.

According to our charts, we were nearing the coasts of Mernadin. We posted more lookouts, arranged the fleets of Humanity in battle order, checked our armament and cut our speed.

The morning passed slowly as we waited, the flagship in the forefront rocking on the waves, its sails reefed, its oars raised.

And then, around noon, the lookout in our topmast yelled through his megaphone:

"Ships for'ard! Five sails!"

King Rigenos, Katorn and I stood on the foredeck, staring ahead. I looked at King Rigenos and frowned. "Five ships? Five ships only?"

King Rigenos shook his head. "Perhaps they are not Eldren ships."

"They'll be Eldren craft," Katorn grunted. "What else could they be in these waters? No human merchants would trade with the creatures!"

And then the cry of the lookout reached us again.

"Ten sails now! Twenty! It's the fleet—the Eldren fleet! They are sailing fast upon us!"

And now I thought I glimpsed a flash of white on the horizon. Had it been the crest of a wave? No. It was the sail of a ship, I was sure.

"Look," I said. "There." And I pointed.

Rigenos screwed up his eyes and shielded them with his hand. "I see nothing. It is your imagination. They could not be coming in so fast."

Katorn, too, peered ahead. "Yes! I see it, too. A sail! They are that swift! By the Sea God's scales—slimy sorcery aids them! It is the only explanation."

King Rigenos seemed sceptical. "They are lighter craft than ours," he reminded Katorn, "and the wind is in their favour."

Katorn, in turn, was not convinced. "Maybe," he growled. "Perhaps you are right, sire."

"Have they used sorcery before?" I asked him. I was willing to believe anything. I had to if I was to believe what had happened to me!

"Aye!" spat Katorn. "Many times. All kinds! Ooph! I can smell sorcery on the very air!"

"When?" I asked him. "What kind? I wish to know so that I can take counter-measures."

"They can make themselves invisible sometimes. That's how they took Paphanaal, so it's said. They can walk on water, sail through the air."

"You have seen them do this?"

"Not myself. But I've heard many tales, tales I can believe from men who do not lie."

"And these men have experienced this sorcery?"

"Not themselves. But they have known men who did."

"So their use of sorcery remains a rumour," I said.

"Ach! Say what you like!" Katorn roared. "Do not believe me— you who are the very essence of sorcery, who owes his existence to an incantation. Why do you think I supported the notion to bring you back, Erekosë? Because I felt we needed sorcery that would be stronger than theirs! What else is that sword at your side but a sorcerous blade?"

I shrugged. "Let us wait, then," I said, "and see their sorcery."

King Rigenos called up at the lookout. "How big's the fleet you see?"

"About half our size, my liege!" he shouted back, his words distorted by the megaphone. "Certainly no larger. And I think it is their whole fleet. I see no more coming."

"They do not seem to be drawing any closer at this moment," I murmured to King Rigenos. "Ask him if they're moving."

"Has the Eldren fleet hove to, master lookout?" called King Rigenos.

"Aye, my liege. It no longer speeds hither and they seem to be furling their sails."

"They are waiting for us," Katorn muttered. "They want us to attack them. Well, we shall wait, too."

I nodded. "That is the strategy we agreed."

And we waited.

We waited as the sun set and night fell and far away on the horizon we caught the occasional glimpse of silver that could have been a wave or a ship. Hasty messages were sent by swimmers back and forth among the vessels of the fleet.

And we continued to wait, sleeping as best we could, wondering when, if at all, the Eldren would attack.

Katorn's footsteps could be heard pacing the deck as I lay awake in my cabin, trying to do the sensible thing and preserve my energy for the next day. Of all of us, Katorn was the most impatient to engage the enemy. I felt that, if it had been up to him, we should even now be sailing on the Eldren, having thrown our carefully worked-out battle plans overboard.

But luckily it was up to me. Even King Rigenos did not have the authority, except under exceptional circumstances, to countermand any of my orders.

I rested, but I could not sleep. I had had my first glimpse of an Eldren craft, yet I still did not know what the ships really looked like or what my impression of their crews would be.

I lay there, praying that our battle should soon begin. A fleet of only half our size! I smiled without humour. I smiled because I knew we should be victorious.

When would the Eldren attack?

It might even be tonight. Katorn had said that they loved the night.

I would not care if it was at night. I wanted to fight. A huge battle-lust was building within me. I wanted to fight!

II

THE FLEETS ENGAGE

A WHOLE DAY passed and another night and still the Eldren remained on the horizon.

Were they deliberately hoping to tire us, make us nervous? Or were they afraid of the size of our fleet? Perhaps, I thought, their own strategy depended on our attacking them.

On the second night I did sleep, but not the drink-sodden slumber I had trained myself to. There was no drink left. Count Roldero had never had a chance to bring his wineskins on board.

And the dreams, if anything, were worse than ever.

I saw entire worlds at war, destroying themselves in senseless battles.

I saw Earth, but this was an Earth without a moon, an Earth which did not rotate, which was half in sunlight, half in a darkness relieved only by the stars. And there was strife here, too, and a morbid quest that as good as destroyed me. A name—Clarvis? Something of the sort. I grasped at these names, but they almost always eluded me and, I suppose, they were really the least important parts of the dreams.

I saw Earth—a different Earth again, an Earth which was so old that even the seas had begun to dry up. And I rode across a murky landscape, beneath a tiny sun, and I thought about Time.

I tried to hang on to this dream, this hallucination, this memory, whatever it was. I thought there might be a clue here to what I was, what had begun it all.

Another name—the Chronarch. Then it faded. There seemed to be no extra significance to this dream than to the rest.

Then this dream had faded and I stood in a city beside a large car and I was laughing and there was a strange sort of gun in my hand and bombs were raining from planes and destroying the city. I tasted an Upmann cigar.

I woke up, but was almost at once dragged back into my dreams.

I walked, insane and lonely, through corridors of steel and beyond the walls of the corridors was empty space. Earth was far behind. The steel machine in which I paced was heading for another star. I was tormented. I was obsessed with thoughts of my family. John Daker? No—John.

And then, as if to confuse me further, the names began. I saw them. I heard them. They were spelled in many different forms of hieroglyphics, chanted in many tongues.

Aubec. Byzantium. Cornelius. Colvin. Bradbury. London. Melniboné. Hawkmoon. Lanjis Liho. Powys. Marca. Elric. Muldoon. Dietrich. Arflane. Simon. Kane. Begg. Corum. Persson. Ryan. Asquiol. Pepin. Seward. Mennell. Tallow. Hallner. Köln. Carnelian. Bastable. Von Bek...

The names went on and on and on.

I awoke screaming.

And it was morning.

Sweating, I got out of my bunk and splashed cold water all over my body.

Why did it not begin? Why?

I knew that, once the fighting started, the dreams would go away. I was sure of it.

And then the door of my cabin burst open and a slave entered.

"Master—"

A trumpet voiced a brazen bellow. There were the sounds of running men all over the ship.

"Master, the enemy ships are moving."

With a great sigh of relief I dressed myself, buckling on my armour as quickly as I could and strapping my sword about me.

Then I ran up on deck and climbed to the forecastle where King Rigenos stood, clad in his own armour, his face grim.

Everywhere in the fleet the war signals were being flown and voices called from ship to ship, trumpets snarled like metallic beasts and drums began to beat.

Now I could see for certain that the Eldren ships were on the move.

"Our commanders are all prepared," Rigenos murmured tensely. "See, our ships are already taking their positions."

I looked with pleasure as the fleet began to form itself according to our much rehearsed battle plan. Now, if only the Eldren would behave as we had anticipated, we should be the victors.

I looked forward again and gasped as the Eldren ships drew closer, marvelled at their rare grace as they leaped lightly over the water like dolphins.

But they were not dolphins, I thought. They would rend us all if they could. Now I understood something of Katorn's suspicion of everything Eldren. If I had not known that these were our enemies, that they intended to destroy us, I would have stood there entranced at their beauty.

They were not galleons, as most of our craft were. They were ships of sail only—and the sails were diaphanous on slim masts. White hulls broke the darker white of the surf as they surged wildly, without faltering, towards us.

I studied their armament intently.

They mounted some cannon, but not as many as ours. Their cannon, however, were slender and silver and, when I saw them, I feared their power.

Katorn joined us. He was snarling with pleasure. "Ah, now," he growled. "Now. Now. See their guns, Erekosë? Beware of them. There is sorcery, if you do not believe me!"

"Sorcery? What do you mean?"

But he was off again, shouting at the men in the rigging to hurry their work.

I began to make out tiny figures on the decks of the Eldren ships. I caught glimpses of eldritch faces, but still could not, at that distance, discern any special characteristics. They moved swiftly about their ships as they swam speedily towards us.

Now our own fleet's manoeuvres were almost complete and the flagship began to move into position.

I myself gave the orders to heave to and we rocked in the sea, awaiting the Eldren ships rushing towards us.

As planned, we had manoeuvred to form a square that was strong on three sides, but weak on the side facing the Eldren fleet.

Some hundred ships were at the far end of the square, set stem to stern with cannon bristling. The two other strong sides also had about a hundred ships each and were at a far enough distance from each other so that their cannon could not accidentally sink one of their own craft. We had placed a thinner wall of ships—about twenty-five—at the side of the square where the Eldren were drawing in. We hoped to give the impression of a tightly closed square formation, with a few ships in the middle flying the royal colours, to give the impression that this was the flagship and its escorts. These ships were bait. The true flagship—the one on which I stood—had temporarily taken down its colours and lay roughly in the middle of the starboard side of the square.

Closer and closer now the Eldren ships approached. It was almost true what Katorn had said. They did seem to fly through the air rather than through the waves.

My hands began to sweat. Would they take the bait? The plan had struck the commanders as original, which meant that it was not the classical manoeuvre it had been in some periods of Earth's history. If it did not work, I would lose Katorn's confidence still further and it would not make my position any better with the king, whose daughter I hoped to marry.

But there was no point in worrying about that. I watched.

And the Eldren took the bait.

Cannon roaring, the Eldren craft smashed in a delta formation into the thin wall and, under their own impetus, sailed on to find themselves thickly surrounded on three sides.

"Raise our colours!" I shouted to Katorn. "Raise the colours! Let them see the originator of their defeat!"

Katorn gave the orders. My own banner went up first—the black field with the silver sword—and then the king's. We moved to tighten the trap, to crush the Eldren as they realised they had been tricked.

I had never seen such highly manoeuvrable sailing craft as the slender ships used by the Eldren. Slightly smaller than our men-o'-war, they darted about seeking an opening in the wall of ships. But there was no opening. I had seen to that.

Now their cannon bellowed fiercely, gouting balls of flame. Was this what Katorn had meant by "sorcery"? The Eldren ammunition was fire-bombs rather than solid shot of the sort we used. Like comets, the fireballs hurtled through the noonday air. Many of our ships were fired. They blazed, crackling and groaning as the flames consumed them.

Like comets they were and the ships were like flashing sharks.

But they were sharks caught in a net that could not be broken. Inexorably we tightened the trap, our own guns booming heavy iron that tore into those white hulls and left black, gaping wounds; that ripped through those slim masts and brought the yards splintering down, the diaphanous sails flapping and fading like the wings of dying moths.

Our own monstrous men-o'-war, their heavy timbers clothed in brass, their huge oars churning the water, their dark, painted sails bulging, drew in to crush the Eldren.

Then the Eldren fleet divided into two roughly equal parts and dashed for the far corners of the net of ships—its weakest points. Many Eldren craft broke through, but we were prepared for this and with monumental precision our ships closed around them.

The Eldren fleet was now divided into several groups and it made our work easier. Implacably we sailed in to crush them.

The skies were filled with smoke and the seas with flaming wreckage and the air was populated by screams, yells and war-shouts, the whine of the Eldren fireballs, the roar of our own shot, the shattering bellowings of the cannon. My face was covered by a film of grease and ash from the smoke and I sweated in the heat from the flames.

From time to time I caught a glimpse of a tense Eldren face and I wondered at their beauty and feared that perhaps we had been overconfident in our assumption of our victory. They were clad in light armour and moved about their ships as gracefully as trained dancers and their silver cannon did not once pause in their bombardment of our craft. Wherever the fireballs landed, the decks or rigging became instantly alight with a shrieking, all-consuming flame that burned green and blue and seemed to devour metal as easily as it did wood.

I gripped the rail of the foredeck and leaned forward, trying to peer through the stinging smoke. All at once I saw an Eldren ship side-on immediately ahead of us.

"Prepare to ram!" I yelled. "Prepare to ram!"

Like many of our ships, the *Iolinda* possessed an iron-shod ram lying just below the waterline. Now was our chance to use it. I saw the Eldren commander on his poop deck shout orders to his men to turn the ship. But it was too late even for the speedy Eldren. We bore down on the smaller craft and, our whole ship reverberating with the mighty roar, we drove into its side. Iron and timber screamed and ruptured, and foam lashed skyward. I was thrown back against the mast, losing my footing, and, as I clambered to my feet, I saw that we had broken the Eldren craft completely in two. I looked on the sight with a mixture of horror and exultation. I had not guessed the brutal power of the *Iolinda*.

On either side of our flagship I saw the two halves of the enemy ship rear in the water and begin to go down. The horror on my own face seemed matched by that on the Eldren commander's as he fiercely strove to hold himself erect on his sloping poop deck while his men threw up their arms and leaped into the dark, surging sea that was already full of smashed timbers and drifting corpses.

Swiftly now the sea swallowed the slim ship and I heard King Rigenos laughing behind me as the Eldren drowned.

I turned. His face was smeared by soot and his red-rimmed eyes stared wildly out of his haggard skull. The helmet-crown of iron and diamonds was askew on his head as he continued to laugh in his morbid triumph.

"Good work, Erekosë! The most satisfying method of all when

dealing with these creatures. Break them open. Send them to the depths of the ocean so that they can be that much closer to their master, the Lord of Hell!"

Katorn climbed up. His face, too, was exultant. "I'll give you that, Lord Erekosë. You have proved you know how to kill Eldren."

"I know how to kill many kinds of men," I said quietly. I was disgusted by their response. I had admired the way in which the Eldren commander had died. "I merely took an opportunity," I said. "There is nothing clever in a ship of this size crushing lighter craft."

But there was no time to dispute the issue. Our ship was moving through the wreckage it had created, surrounded by orange tongues of flame, shrieks and yells, thick smoke which obscured vision in all directions so that it was impossible to tell how the fleets of Humanity fared.

"We must get out of this," I said. "Into clearer sea. We must let our own ships know that we are unharmed. Will you give the orders, Katorn?"

"Aye." Katorn went back to his duties.

My head was beginning to throb with the din of the battle. It became one great wall of noise, one huge wave of smoke and flame and the stench of death.

And yet—it was all familiar to me.

Up to now my battle tactics had been somewhat notional— intellectual rather than instinctive. But now it did seem that old instincts came into play and I gave orders without working them out first.

And I was confident that the orders were good. Even Katorn trusted them.

Thus it had been with the order to ram the Eldren craft. I had not stopped to think. It was probably just as well.

Its oars pulling strongly, the *Iolinda* cleared the worst of the smoke and her trumpets and drums announced her presence to the rest of the fleet. A cheering went up from some of the nearby ships as we emerged into an area relatively free of smoke, wreckage and other ships.

A few of our craft had begun to single out individual Eldren vessels and were hurling out their grappling irons towards the shark-ships. The savage barbs cut into the white rails, ripped through the shining sails, bit into flesh and tore off arms and legs. The great men-o'-war dragged the Eldren craft towards them, as whalers haul in their half-dead prey.

Arrows began to fly from deck to deck as archers, their legs twisted in the rigging, shot at enemy archers. Javelins rattled on the decks or pierced the armour of the warriors, Eldren and human, and threw them prone. The sound of cannon could still be heard, but it was not the steady pounding it had been. The shots became more intermittent and were replaced by the clash of swords, the shouts of warriors fighting hand to hand.

Smoke still formed acrid blossoms in the air above that watery battlefield. And when I could see through the murk to the green, wreckage-strewn ocean itself, I saw that the foam was no longer white. It was red. The sea was covered by a slick of blood.

As our ship beat on to join battle once again, I saw upturned faces staring at me from the sea. They were the faces of the dead, both Eldren and human, and they seemed to share a common expression—an expression of astonished accusation.

After a while, I tried to ignore the sight of those faces.

∽ 12 ∞

THE BROKEN TRUCE

TWO MORE SHIPS fell to our ram and we sustained hardly any damage at all. The *Iolinda* moved through the battle like a dignified juggernaut, as if assured of her own invulnerability.

It was King Rigenos who saw it first. He screwed up his eyes and pointed through the smoke, his open mouth red in the blackness of his soot-covered face.

"There! See it, Erekosë? There!"

I saw a magnificent Eldren ship ahead of us, but I did not know why Rigenos singled it out.

"It is the Eldren flagship, Erekosë," Rigenos said. "It could be that their leader himself is aboard. If that cursed servant of Azmobaana does ride his own flagship and if we can destroy him, then our cause will be truly won. Pray that the Eldren prince rides her, Erekosë!"

Katorn snarled from behind us: "I would like to be the one to bring him down." He had a heavy crossbow in his mailed hands and he stroked its butt as another man might stroke a favourite kitten.

"Oh, let Prince Arjavh be there. Let him be there," hissed Rigenos thirstily.

I paid them little heed, but shouted the order for grappling irons to be readied.

Luck, it seemed, was still with us. Our huge vessel reared up on a surging wave at exactly the right moment and we rode it down upon the Eldren flagship, our timbers scraping its sides and turning it so that it lay in a perfect position for our grapples to seize it. The iron claws snaked out on thick ropes, clamped in the rigging, stabbed into the deck, snatched at the rails.

Now the Eldren craft was bound to us. We held it close, as a lover holds his mistress.

And that same smile of triumph began to cross my face. I had the sweet taste of victory on my lips. It was the sweetest taste of all. I, Erekosë, signed for a slave to run forward and wipe my face with a damp cloth. I drew myself up proudly on my deck. Just behind me was King Rigenos, on my right. On my left was Katorn. I felt a comradeship with them suddenly. I looked proudly down on the Eldren deck. The warriors looked exhausted. But they stood ready, with arrows strung on bows, with swords clenched in white fists and shields raised. They watched us silently; they did not attempt to cut the ropes, they waited for us to make the first move.

When two flagships locked in this way, there was always a pause before fighting broke out. This was to enable the enemy commanders to speak and, if both desired it, decide a truce and the terms of that truce.

Now King Rigenos bellowed across the rail of his high deck, calling out to the Eldren who looked up at him, their strange eyes smarting with the smoke as much as ours did.

"This is King Rigenos and his champion, the immortal Erekosë, your ancient enemy come again to defeat you. We, would speak with your commander for a moment, in the usual truce".

From beneath a canvas awning on his poop deck, a tall man

now emerged. Through the shifting smoke I saw, dimly at first, a pointed, golden face with blue-flecked milky eyes staring sadly from the sockets of the slanting brow. An eldritch voice, like music, sang across the sea:

"I am Duke Baynahn, commander of the Eldren fleet. We will make no complicated peace terms with you, but if you let us sail away now, we will not continue to fight."

Rigenos smiled and Katorn snorted. "How gracious! He knows he is doomed."

Rigenos chuckled at this. Then he called back to Duke Baynahn.

"I find your proposal somewhat naïve, Duke Baynahn."

Baynahn shrugged wearily. "Then let us finish this," he sighed. He raised his gloved hand to order his men to loose their arrows.

"Hold a moment!" Rigenos shouted. "There is another way, if you would spare your men."

Slowly Baynahn lowered his hand. "What is that?" His voice was wary.

"If your master, Arjavh of Mernadin, is aboard his own flagship—as he should be—let him come out and do battle with Lord Erekosë, Humanity's champion." King Rigenos spread out his palms. "If Arjavh should win, why, you will go in peace. If Erekosë should win, then you will become our prisoners."

Duke Baynahn folded his arms across his chest. "I have to tell you that our Prince Arjavh could not get to Paphanaal in time to sail with our fleet. He is in the west—in Loos Ptokai."

King Rigenos turned to Katorn.

"Kill that one, Katorn," he said quietly.

Duke Baynahn continued: "However, I am prepared to fight your champion if…"

"No!" I cried to Katorn. "Stop! King Rigenos, that is dishonourable—you speak during a truce."

"There is no question of honour, Erekosë, when exterminating vermin. That you will soon learn. Kill him, Katorn!"

Duke Baynahn was frowning, plainly puzzled at our muted argument, striving to catch the words.

"I will fight your Erekosë," he said. "Is it agreed?"

And Katorn brought up the crossbow and the bolt whirred and I heard a soft gasp as it penetrated the Eldren speaker's throat.

His hands went up towards the quivering bolt. His strange eyes filmed. He fell.

I was enraged at the treachery shown by one who so often spoke of treachery in his enemies. But now there was no time to remonstrate for already the Eldren arrows were whistling towards us and I had to ensure our defences and prepare to lead the boarding party against the betrayed crew of the enemy ship.

I grasped a trailing rope, unsheathed my glowing sword and let the words come from my lips, though I was still full of anger against Katorn and the king.

"For Humanity!" I shouted. "Death to the Hounds of Evil!"

I swung down through the heated air that slashed against my face in that swift passage and I dropped, with howling human warriors behind me, among the Eldren ranks.

Then we were fighting.

My followers took care to stay away from me as the sword opened pale wounds in the Eldren foes, destroying all whom it even lightly cut. Many Eldren died beneath Kanajana, but there was no battle-joy in me as I fought, for I was still furious with my own people's actions and there was no skill needed for such slaying—the Eldren were shocked at the death of their commander and they were plainly half-dead with weariness, though they fought bravely.

Indeed, the slender ships seemed to hold more men than I had estimated. The long-skulled Eldren, well aware that my sword touch was lethal, flung themselves at me with desperate and ferocious courage.

Many of them wielded long-hafted axes, swinging at me out of reach of my sword. The sword was no sharper than any ordinary blade and, although I hacked at the shafts, I succeeded only in splintering them slightly. I had constantly to duck, stab beneath the whirling axe blades.

A young, golden-haired Eldren leaped at me, swung his axe and it smashed against my shoulder plate, knocking me off balance.

I rolled, trying desperately to regain my footing on the blood-smeared deck. The axe smashed down again, onto my breastplate, winding me. I struggled up into a crouching position, plunged forward beneath the axe and slashed at the Eldren's bared wrist.

A peculiar sobbing grunt escaped his lips. He groaned and died. The "poison" of the blade had done its work yet again. I still did not understand how the metal itself could be poisoned, but there was no doubting its effectiveness. I straightened up, my bruised body throbbing as I stared down at the brave young Eldren who now lay at my feet. Then I looked about me.

I saw that we had the advantage. The last pocket of fiercely fighting Eldren was on the main deck, back to back around their banner—a scarlet field bearing the silver basilisk of Mernadin.

I stumbled towards the fray. The Eldren were fighting to the last man. They knew they would receive no mercy from their human enemies.

I stopped. The warriors had no need of help from me. I sheathed my sword and watched as the Eldren were engulfed by our forces and, although all badly wounded, continued to fight until slain.

I looked about me. A peculiar silence seemed to surround the two locked ships, though in the distance the sound of cannon could still be heard.

Then Katorn, who had led the attack on the last Eldren defenders, snatched down their basilisk banner and flung it into the flowing Eldren blood. Insanely he began to trample the flag until it was completely soaked and unrecognizable.

"Thus will all the Eldren perish!" he screamed in his mad triumph. "All! All! All!"

He stumbled below to see what loot there was.

The silence returned. The drifting smoke began to dissipate and hang higher in the air above us, obscuring the sunlight.

Now that the flagship was ours, the day was won. Not a single prisoner would be taken. In the distance the victorious human warriors were busy firing the Eldren vessels. There seemed to be no Eldren ships left uncaptured, none fleeing over the horizon. Many of our own ships had been destroyed or were sinking in flames. Both sides' craft were stretched across a vast expanse of water and the ocean itself was covered by so great and thick a carpet of wreckage and corpses that it seemed as if the remaining ships were embedded in it.

I, for one, felt trapped by it. I wanted to leave this scene as soon as possible. The smell of the dead choked me. This was not the battle I had expected to fight. This was not the glory I had hoped to win.

Katorn re-emerged with a look of satisfaction on his dark face.

"You're empty-handed," I said. "Why so pleased?"

He wiped his lips. "Duke Baynahn had his daughter with him."

"Is she still alive?"

"Not now."

I shuddered.

Katorn stretched up his head and looked around him. "Good. We've finished them. I'll give orders to fire the remaining vessels."

"Surely," I said, "that is a waste. We could use their ships to replace those we have lost."

"Use these cursed craft? Never." He spoke with a twist of his mouth and strode to the rail of the Eldren flagship, shouting to his men to follow him back to their own vessel.

I came reluctantly, looking back to where the corpse of the betrayed Duke Baynahn still lay, the crossbow bolt projecting from his slender neck.

Then I clambered aboard our ship and I gave the orders to save what grapples we could and cut away the rest.

King Rigenos greeted me. He had taken no part in the actual fighting. "You did well, Erekosë. Why, you could have taken that ship single-handed."

"I could have," I said. "I could have taken the whole fleet single-handed."

He laughed. "You are very confident! The whole fleet!"

"Aye. There was one way."

He frowned. "What do you mean?"

"If you had let me fight Duke Baynahn—as he suggested— many lives and many ships would have been saved. Our lives. Our ships."

"You surely did not trust him? The Eldren will always try some trick like that. Doubtless, if you had agreed to his plan, you would have stepped aboard his ship and been cut down by a hundred arrows. Believe me, Erekosë, you must not be deceived by them. Our ancestors were so deceived—and look how we suffer now."

I shrugged. "Maybe you are right."

"Of course I am right." King Rigenos turned his head and called to our crew. "Fire the ship! Fire that cursed Eldren craft! Hurry, you laggards!"

He was in a good humour was King Rigenos. A great good humour.

I watched as blazing arrows were accurately shot into bales of combustible materials which had been placed in strategic parts of the Eldren ship.

The slender vessel soon caught. The bodies of the slain began to burn and oily smoke struck upward to the sky. The ship drifted away, its silver cannon like the snouts of slaughtered beasts, its glistening sails dropping in flaming ribbons to the already flaming deck. It gave a long shudder suddenly as if expiring the last of its life.

"Put a couple of shots below the waterline," Katorn shouted to his gunners. "Let's make sure the thing sinks once and for all."

Our brazen cannon snarled and the heavy shot smashed into the Eldren flagship, sending up gouts of water and crashing through the timbers.

The flagship yawed, but still seemed to be trying to stay upright. Her drifting went slower and slower as she settled lower in the water until she had stopped altogether. And then all at once she sank swiftly and was gone.

I thought of the Eldren duke. I thought of his daughter.

And something in me envied them. They would know eternal peace, just as it seemed I should know nothing but eternal strife.

Our fleet began to reassemble.

We had lost thirty-eight men-o'-war and a hundred and ten smaller craft of different types.

But nothing remained of the Eldren fleet.

Nothing but the burning hulks which we left, sinking, behind us as we sailed, in battle-thirsty glee, for Paphanaal.

∽ 13 ∾

PAPHANAAL

FOR THE REST of our sailing towards Paphanaal, I avoided both Katorn and King Rigenos. Perhaps they were right and the Eldren could not be trusted. But should we not set some kind of example?

On the second night of the voyage after the big battle with the Eldren, Count Roldero visited me.

"You did well there," he said. "Your tactics were superb. And I hear you accounted well for yourself in the hand-to-hand fighting." He looked about him in mock fear and whispered, jerking his thumb at a vague spot above him, "But I hear Rigenos decided that it was best he did not put the royal person in danger, lest we warriors lose heart."

"Oh," I said, "Rigenos has a fair point. He came with us, don't forget. He could have stayed behind. We all expected him to. Did you hear of the order he gave while the truce was on with the enemy commander?"

Roldero sniffed. "Had him shot by Katorn?"

"Yes."

"Well…" Roldero grinned at me. "You make allowances for Rigenos's cowardice and I'll make allowances for his treachery!"

He burst into gusty laughter. "That's fair, eh?"

I could not help smiling. But later, more seriously, I said: "Would you have done the same, Roldero?"

"Oh, I expect so. War, after all…"

"But Baynahn was prepared to fight me. He must have known his chances were slim. He must have known, too, that Rigenos could not be trusted to keep his word."

"If he did, then he would have acted as Rigenos acted. It was just that Rigenos was quicker. Merely tactics, you see—the trick is to gauge the exact moment to be treacherous."

"Baynahn did not look like one who would have acted treacherously."

"He was probably a very kind man and treated his family well. I told you, Erekosë, it is not Baynahn's character I dispute. I just say that, as a warrior, he would have tried what Rigenos succeeded in doing—eliminating the enemy's chief. It is one of the basic principles of warfare!"

"Do you say so, Roldero?"

"I do say so. Now drink up."

I did drink up. And I drank deep and I drank myself stupid. Now there were not merely the dream memories to contend with, but much more recent memories, too.

Another night came before we reached the harbour city of Paphanaal and we lay at anchor, a sea league or so offshore.

Then, in the shifting dawn of the morrow, we upped anchors and rowed in towards Paphanaal, for there was no wind to fill our sails.

Nearer we came to land.

I saw cliffs and black mountains rising.

Nearer.

I saw a flash of brighter colour to the east of us.

"*Paphanaal!*" shouted the lookout from his precarious perch in the top trees.

Nearer.

And there was Paphanaal.

She was undefended as far as we could make out. We had left her defenders on the bottom of the ocean, far behind.

There were no domes on this city, no minarets. There were steeples and buttresses and battlements, all close together. They made the city seem like one great palace. The materials of their construction were breathtaking. There was white marble veined with pink, blue, green and yellow. Orange marble, veined with black. Marble faced with gold, basalt and quartz and bluestone in abundance.

It was a shining city.

As we came closer, we saw no one on the quaysides, no one in the streets or on the battlements. I assumed that the city had been deserted.

I was wrong.

We put in to the great harbour and disembarked. I formed our armies into disciplined ranks and warned them of a possible trap, although I did not really believe there could be one.

The warriors had spent the rest of the voyage repairing their clothes and their armour, cleaning their weapons and making repairs to their ships.

All the ships crowded the harbour now, their flags waving in the light breeze that had come up almost as soon as we set foot on the cobblestones of the quay. Clouds came in with the breeze and made the day grey.

The warriors stood before King Rigenos, Katorn and myself. Rank upon rank they stood, their armour bright, their heavy banners moving sluggishly.

There were seven hundred divisions, each hundred divisions commanded by a marshal, who had as his commanders his captains, who controlled twenty-five divisions each, and his knights, who controlled one division.

The wine had helped fade the memory of the battle and I felt the return of my old pride as I stood looking at the paladins and armies of Humanity assembled before me. I addressed them.

"Marshals, Captains, Knights and Warriors of Humanity, you have seen me to be a victorious war leader."

"Aye!" they roared, jubilant.

"We shall be victorious here and elsewhere in the land of Mernadin. Go now, with caution, and search these buildings for Eldren. But be careful. This city could hide an army, remember!"

Count Roldero spoke up from the front rank.

"And booty, Lord Erekosë. What of that?"

King Rigenos waved his hand. "Take what booty you desire. But remember what Erekosë has said—be wary for such things as poisoned food. Even the wine-cups could be smeared with poison. Anything in this damned city could be poisoned!"

The divisions began to march past us, each taking a different direction.

I watched them go and I thought that, while the city received them into its heart, it did not welcome them.

I wondered what we would find in Paphanaal. Traps? Hidden snipers? Everything poisoned, as Rigenos had said?

* * *

We found a city of women.

Not one Eldren man had remained.

Not one boy over twelve. Not one old man of any age.

We had slain them all at sea.

~3 **14** ~c

ERMIZHAD

I DID NOT know how they slew the children. I begged King
Rigenos not to give the order. I pleaded with Katorn to spare
them—to drive them from the city if he must, but not to kill them.

But the children were slain. I do not know how many.

We had taken over the palace which had belonged to Duke
Baynahn himself. He had, it transpired, been warden of
Paphanaal.

I shut myself in my quarters while the slaughter went on
outside. I reflected sardonically that for all their talk of the Eldren
"filth", they did not seem to mind forcing their attentions on the
Eldren women.

There was nothing I could do. I did not even know if there
was anything I should do. I had been brought here by Rigenos
to fight for Humanity, not to judge it. I had agreed to answer his
summons, after all—doubtless with reason. But I had forgotten
any reason.

I sat in a room that was exquisitely furnished with delicate furniture and fine, light tapestries on walls and floor. I looked at the Eldren craftsmanship and I sipped the aromatic Eldren wine and I tried not to listen to the cries of the Eldren children as they were butchered in their beds in the houses in the streets beyond the thin palace walls.

I looked at Kanajana, which I had propped in a corner, and I hated the poisoned thing. I had stripped myself of my armour and I sat alone.

And I drank more wine.

But the wine of the Eldren began to taste of blood and I tossed the cup away and found a skin that Count Roldero had given me and sucked it dry of the bitter wine it contained.

But I could not get drunk. I could not stop the screams from the streets. I could not fail to see the flickering shadows on the tapestries I had drawn over the windows. I could not get drunk and therefore I could not even begin to try to sleep, for I knew what my dreams would be and I feared those almost as much as I feared thinking of the implications of what we were doing to those who were left in Paphanaal.

Why was I here? Oh, why was I here?

There was a noise outside my door and then a knock.

"Enter," I said.

No one entered. My voice had been too low.

The knock sounded again.

I rose and walked unsteadily to the door and flung it open.

"Can you not leave me in peace?"

A frightened soldier of the Imperial Guard stood there. "Lord Erekosë, forgive me for disturbing you, but I bear a message from King Rigenos."

"What's the message?" I said without interest.

"He would like you to join him. He says that there are still plans to discuss."

I sighed. "Very well. I will come down shortly."

The soldier hurried off along the corridor.

At last, reluctantly, I rejoined the other conquerors. All the marshals were there, lounging on cushions and celebrating their victory. King Rigenos was there and he was so drunk that I envied him. And, to my relief, Katorn was not there.

Doubtless he was leading the looters.

As I came into the hall, a huge cheer went up from the marshals and they raised their wine-cups in a toast to me.

I ignored them and walked to where the king was seated alone, staring vacantly into space.

"You wish to discuss further campaigns, King Rigenos," I said. "Are you sure?"

"Ah, my friend Erekosë. The Immortal. The Champion. The saviour of Humanity. Greetings, Erekosë." He put a hand drunkenly on my arm. "You disapprove of my unkingly insobriety, I see."

"I disapprove of nothing," I said. "I have been drinking much myself."

"But you—an Immortal—can contain your—" he belched— "can contain your liquor."

I took pains to smile and said: "Perhaps you have stronger liquor. If so, let me try it."

"Slave!" screamed King Rigenos. "Slave! More of that wine for my friend Erekosë!"

A curtain parted and a trembling Eldren boy appeared. He was bearing a wineskin almost as large as himself.

"I see you have not slain all the children," I said.

King Rigenos giggled. "Not yet. Not while there are uses for them!"

I took the wineskin from the child and nodded to him. "You may go." I held the skin and put the opening to my lips and began to drink deeply. But still the wine refused to dull my brain. I hurled the skin away and it fell heavily and slopped wine over the tapestries and cushions covering the floor.

King Rigenos continued to giggle. "Good! Good!"

These people were barbarians. Suddenly I wished that I was John Daker again. Studious, unhappy John Daker, living his quiet, cut-off life in the pursuit of pointless learning.

I turned to leave.

"Stay, Erekosë. I'll sing a song. It's a filthy song about the filthy Eldren."

"Tomorrow."

"It's already tomorrow!"

"I must rest."

"I am your king, Erekosë. You owe your material form to me. Do not forget that!"

"I have not forgotten."

The doors of the hall burst open then and they dragged in the girl.

Katorn led them and he was grinning like a sated wolf.

She was a black-haired girl. Her alien features were composed against the fear she felt. She had a strange, shifting beauty which was always there but which seemed to change with every breath she took. They had torn her garments and bruised her arms and face.

"Erekosë!" Katorn followed his men in. He, too, was very drunk. "Erekosë—Rigenos, my lord king—*look*!"

The king blinked and looked at the girl with distaste. "Why should we take interest in an Eldren wanton? Get hence, Katorn. Use her as you will—that is your private decision—but be sure she is not still alive when we leave Paphanaal."

"No!" laughed Katorn. "Look! Look at her!"

The king shrugged and inspected the wine swilling in his cup. "Why have you brought her here, Katorn?" I asked quietly.

Katorn rocked with laughter. His thick lips opened wide and he roared in our faces. "You know not who she is, that's plain!"

"Take the Eldren wench away, Katorn!" The king's voice rose in drunken irritation.

"My lord king—this—this is *Ermizhad*!"

"What?" The king leaned forward and stared at the girl. "What? Ermizhad, that whore! Ermizhad of the Ghost Worlds!"

Katorn nodded. "The same."

The king grew more sober. "She's lured many a mortal to his death, so I've heard. She shall die by torture for her lustful crimes. The stake shall have her."

Katorn shook his head. "No, King Rigenos—at least, not yet. Forget you that she's Prince Arjavh's *sister*?"

The king nodded in a mockery of gravity. "Of course. Arjavh's sister."

"And the implications, my lord? We should keep her prisoner, should we not? She will make a good hostage, eh? A good bargaining counter, should we need one?"

"Ah, of course. Yes. You did right, Katorn. Keep her prisoner." The king grinned a silly grin. "No. It is not fair. You deserve to enjoy yourself further this night. Who does not wish to enjoy himself?" He looked at me. "Erekosë—Erekosë who cannot get drunk. She shall be put in your charge, Champion."

I nodded. "I accept the charge," I said. I pitied the girl, whatever terrible crimes she had committed.

Katorn looked at me suspiciously.

"Do not worry, Lord Katorn," I said. "Do as the king says— continue to enjoy yourself. Slay some more. Rape some more. There must be plenty left."

Katorn drew his brows together. Then his face cleared a little.

"A few maybe," he said. "But we've been thorough. Only she will live to see the sun rise, I think." He jabbed a thumb at his prisoner, then signed to his men. "Come! Let's finish our task."

He stalked out.

Count Roldero got up slowly and came towards me as I stood looking at the Eldren girl.

The king looked up. "Good. Keep her from harm, Erekosë," he said cynically. "Keep her from harm. She'll be a useful piece in our game with Arjavh."

"Take her to my apartments in the east wing," I told the guards, "and make sure she's unmolested and has no chance to escape."

They took her away and, almost as soon as she had left, King Rigenos made to stand up, swayed and fell with a crash to the floor.

Count Roldero gave a slight smile. "Our liege is not himself," he said. "But Katorn is right. The Eldren bitch will be useful to us."

"I understand her usefulness as a hostage," I said, "but I do not understand this reference to 'the Ghost Worlds'. I've heard them spoken of once before. What are they, Roldero?"

"The Ghost Worlds? Why, we all know of them. I should have thought that you would, too. But we do not often speak of them."

"Why so?"

"Humankind fear Arjavh's allies so much that they will rarely mention them, in terror of conjuring them up by their words, you understand."

"I do not understand."

Roldero rubbed his nose and coughed. "I am not superstitious, Erekosë," he said. "Like yourself."

"I know. But what are the Ghost Worlds?"

Roldero seemed nervous. "I'll tell you, but I'm uncomfortable about doing so in this cursed place. The Eldren know better than we what the Ghost Worlds are. We had thought, at first, that you yourself were a prisoner there. That was why I was surprised."

"Where are they?"

"The Ghost Worlds lie beyond Earth—beyond Time and beyond Space—linked to Earth only by the most tenuous of bonds."

Roldero's voice dropped, but he whispered on.

"There, on the torn Ghost Worlds, dwell the many-coiled serpents which are the terror and the scourge of the eight dimensions. Here, also, live ghosts and men—those who are manlike and those who are unlike men—those who know that their fate is to live without Time, and those who are unaware of their doom. And there, also, do kinfolk to the Eldren dwell—the halflings."

"But what *are* these worlds?" I asked impatiently.

Roldero licked his lips. "They are the worlds to which human sorcerers sometimes go in search of alien wisdom, and from which they draw helpers of horrible powers and disgusting deeds. It is said that within those worlds an initiate may meet his long-slain comrades, who may sometimes help him; his dead loves and his dead kin, and particularly his enemies—those whom he has caused to die. Malevolent enemies with great powers—or wretches who are half-souled and incomplete."

His whispered words convinced me, perhaps because I had drunk so much. Was it these Ghost Worlds that were the origin of my strange dreams? I wanted to know more.

"But what are they, Roldero? Where are they?"

Roldero shook his head. "I do not concern myself with such mysteries, Erekosë. I have never been much of a mystic. I believe—but I do not probe. I know of no answer to either of your questions. They are worlds full of shadow and gloomy shores upon which drab seas beat. The populace can sometimes be summoned by powerful sorcery to visit this Earth, to haunt, to help—or to terrorise. We think that the Eldren came, originally, from these half-worlds if they were not, as our legends say, spawned from the womb of a wicked queen who gave her virginity to Azmobaana in return for immortality—the immortality which her offspring inherited. But the Eldren are material enough, for all their lack of souls, whereas the Ghost Armies are rarely solid flesh."

"And Ermizhad?"

"The Wanton of the Ghost Worlds."

"Why is she called that?"

"It is said that she mates with ghouls," muttered Count Roldero. He shrugged and drank more wine. "And in return for giving her favours to them, she receives special powers over the halflings who are friends with the ghouls. The halflings love her, I'm told, as far as it's possible for such creatures to love."

I could not believe it. The girl seemed young. Innocent. I said as much.

Roldero gestured dismissively. "How do you tell the age of an Immortal? Look at yourself. How old are you, Erekosë? Thirty? You look no older."

"But I have not lived for ever," I said. "At least, not in one body, I do not think."

"But how do you tell?"

I could not answer him, of course. "Well, I think there's a great deal of superstition mixed up in your tale, Roldero," I said. "I would not have expected it of you, old friend."

"Believe me or not," Roldero muttered. "But you would do better to believe me until I am proved a liar, eh?"

"Possibly you're right."

"I sometimes wonder at you, Erekosë," he said. "Here you are owing your own existence to an incantation, and you are the most sceptical man I know!"

I smiled at this. "Yes, Roldero. I should indeed believe more."

"Come," said Roldero, moving towards the prone king, who lay on his face in a pool of wine. "Let's get our lord to bed before he drowns."

Together we picked up the king and called for a soldier to help us as we hauled Rigenos up the stairs and dumped him on his bed.

Roldero put a huge hand on my shoulder. "And stop brooding, friend. It will do no good. Think you that I enjoy the slaughter of children? The rape of young girls?" He rubbed his mouth with the back of his hand as if to rid it of a foul taste. "But if it is not done now, Erekosë, it will be done at some time to our children and to our young girls. I know the Eldren are beautiful. But so are many snakes. So are some kinds of wolf that prey on sheep. It is braver to do what has to be done than it is to pretend to yourself that you are not doing it. You follow me?"

We stood in the king's bedchamber staring at each other.

"You are very kind, Roldero," I said.

"It's well-meant advice," he told me.

"I know it is."

"It was not your decision to slaughter the children," he said.

"But it was my decision to say little of it to King Rigenos," I replied.

At the mention of his name, the king stirred and began to mumble in his stupor.

"Come," grinned Roldero. "Let's get out of here before he remembers the words of that dirty song he promised to sing us."

We parted in the corridor outside the chamber. Count Roldero looked at me with some concern. "These actions must be made," he said. "It has befallen us to be the instruments of a decision made some centuries ago. Do not bother yourself with matters of conscience. The future may see us as bloody-handed butchers. But we know we are not. We are men. We are warriors. And we are at war with those who would destroy us."

I said nothing, but put my hand on his shoulder, then turned and walked back to my lonely apartments.

In my mental discomfort, I had all but forgotten the girl until I saw the guard at my door.

"Is the prisoner secure?" I asked him.

"There is no way out," the guard said. "No way, at least, Lord Erekosë, that a human could take. But if she were to summon her halfling allies…"

"We'll concern ourselves with those when they materialise," I told him. He unlocked the door for me and I entered.

There was only one lamp burning and I could barely see. I took a taper from a table and with it lit another lamp.

The Eldren girl lay on the bed. Her eyes were closed, but her cheeks were stained with tears.

So they cry like us, too, I thought.

I tried not to disturb her, but she opened her eyes and I thought I saw fear in them, though it was difficult to tell, for the eyes really were strange—without orbs and flecked with gold and blue. Seeing those eyes, I remembered what Roldero had told me and I began to believe him.

"How are you?" I asked inanely.

Her lips parted, but she did not speak.

"I do not intend to harm you," I said weakly. "I would have spared the children if I could. I would have spared the warriors in the battle. But I have only the power to lead men to kill each other. I have no power to save their lives."

She frowned.

"I am Erekosë," I said.

"Erekosë?" The name was music when she spoke it. She pronounced it more familiarly than I did myself.

"You know who I am?"

"I know who you were."

"I am reborn," I said. "Do not ask me how."

"You do not seem happy to be reborn, Erekosë."

I shrugged.

"Erekosë," she said again. And then she voiced a low, bitter laugh.

"Why do you laugh?"

But she would not speak again. I tried to converse with her further. She closed her eyes. I left the room and went to the bed next door.

The wine had worked at last—or something had—for I slept without dreaming.

∽ 15 ∾

THE RETURNING

NEXT MORNING I arose, washed myself, dressed and knocked on Ermizhad's door.

There was no reply.

Thinking that she had, perhaps, escaped and that Katorn would be instantly suspicious that I had helped her, I flung open the door and entered.

She had not escaped. She still lay on the bed, but now her eyes were open again as she stared at the ceiling. Those eyes were as mysterious to me as the star-flecked depths of the universe.

"Did you sleep well?" I asked.

She did not reply.

"Are you ill?" was my next, rather stupid question. But she had plainly decided to communicate with me no further. I made one last attempt and then left, going down to the great hall. Here Roldero was waiting for me and there were a few other marshals, looking the worse for wear, but King Rigenos and Katorn were not present.

Roldero's eyes twinkled. "There are no drums beating in your skull by the look of you."

He was right. I had not considered it, but I suffered no aftereffects from the huge quantities of wine drunk the night before.

"I feel very good," I said.

"Ah, now I believe you are an Immortal!" he laughed. "I have not escaped so lightly. Neither, it seems, have King Rigenos and Lord Katorn, or some of the others who were enjoying themselves so much last night." He drew closer and said quietly: "And I hope you are in better spirits today, my friend."

"I suppose that I am," I said. I felt drained of emotion, in fact.

"Good. And what of that Eldren creature? Still safe?"

"Still safe."

"She did not try to seduce you?"

"On the contrary, she will not speak to me at all!"

"Just as well." Roldero looked around impatiently. "I hope they get up soon. There's much to discuss. Do we carry on inland or what?"

"I thought we agreed that the best plan was to leave a good force here, strong enough to defend the city, and get back to the Two Continents to re-equip and to check any attempt to invade us while our fleet's at Paphanaal."

Roldero nodded. "It's the most sensible plan. But I do not like it very much. While it has logic, it does not suit my impatience to get at the enemy as soon as possible."

I agreed with him. "I would like to have done with this as soon as I am able," I told him.

But we had little clear idea where the rest of the Eldren forces were marshaled. There were four other major cities on the continent of Mernadin. The chief of these was Loos Ptokai, which lay near to the Plains of Melting Ice. This was Arjavh's headquarters and, from what the Eldren on the flagship had said, he was either there now or marching to recapture Paphanaal. It seemed to us that he would attempt this, because Paphanaal was the most important position on the coast. With it in our hands, we had a good harbour in which to bring our ships and land our men.

And if Arjavh did march against us, then all we had to do was save our energy and wait. We thought that we could leave our main force in Paphanaal, return to our own base at Noonos, bringing back the divisions of warriors who, because of insufficient ships, had been unable to come with us on the preliminary expedition.

But Roldero had something else on his mind. "We must not forget the sorcerous fortresses of the Outer Islands," he told me. "They lie at World's Edge. The Outer Islands should be taken as soon as possible."

"What exactly are the Outer Islands? Why are they so strategic?" I asked him. "And why haven't they been mentioned before in our plans?"

"Ah," said Count Roldero. "Ah, it is because of our reluctance, particularly when at home, to discuss the Ghost Worlds."

I made a sign of mock despair. "The Ghost Worlds again!"

"The Outer Islands lie in the gateway to the Ghost Worlds," Roldero said seriously. "From there the Eldren can summon their ghoulish allies. Perhaps, now Paphanaal is taken, we should concentrate on smashing their strength in the west—at World's Edge."

Had I been wrong to be so sceptical? Or was Roldero overestimating the power of the Ghost World denizens? "Roldero, have you ever seen these halflings?" I asked him.

"Oh, yes, my friend," he replied. "You are wrong if you believe them legendary beings. They are, in one sense, real enough."

I became more convinced. I trusted Roldero's opinions more than most.

"Then perhaps we should alter our strategy slightly," I said. "We can leave the main army here to wait for Arjavh to march against the city and waste his strength trying to take it from the land side. We return to Noonos with the large portion of the fleet, add any new ships that are ready to our force, take fresh warriors aboard—and sail against the Outer Islands while, if we are right, Arjavh expends his own force trying to retake Paphanaal."

Roldero nodded. "It seems a wise plan to me, Erekosë. But what of the girl, our hostage? How shall we use her to our best advantage?"

I frowned. I did not like the idea of using her at all. I wondered where she would be safest.

"I suppose we should keep her as far away from here as possible," I said. "Necranal would be best. There is little chance of her people being able to rescue her and she would have a difficult time getting back if she managed to escape. What do you think?"

Roldero nodded. "I think you are right. That's sensible."

"We must discuss all this with the king, of course," I said gravely.

"Of course," said Roldero, and winked.

"And Katorn," I added.

"And Katorn," he agreed. "Especially Katorn."

It was well after noon before we had the chance to speak with Katorn or the king. Both were pale-faced and were quick to agree with our suggestions as if they would agree to anything as long as they were left alone.

"We'll establish our position here," I told the king, "and set sail back to Noonos within the week. We should waste no time. Now that we have gained Paphanaal, we can expect savage counter-attacks from the Eldren."

"Aye," muttered Katorn. He was red-eyed. "And you are right to try to block off Arjavh's summoning of his frightful Ghost Armies."

"I am glad you approve of my plan, Lord Katorn," I said.

His smile was twisted. "You're proving yourself, my lord, after all. Still a little soft towards our enemies, but you're beginning to realise what they're like."

"I wonder," I said.

There were minor details of the plan to discuss and, while the victorious warriors continued to pleasure themselves on Eldren spoils, we talked of these matters until they were completely settled.

It was a good plan.

It would work if the Eldren reacted as we expected. And we were sure that they would.

We agreed that King Rigenos and I would return with the fleet, leaving Katorn to command the army at Paphanaal. Roldero also elected to return with us. The bulk of the warriors would remain behind. We had to hope that the Eldren did not have another fleet in the vicinity, for we would be sailing back with just the minimum crews and would be hard-pressed to defend ourselves if attacked at sea.

But there were risks to all the different possibilities and we had to decide which actions the Eldren were most likely to take and act accordingly.

The next few days were spent in preparation for the voyage back and soon we were ready to sail.

We sailed out of Paphanaal on a dawn tide, our ships moving sluggishly through the water, for they groaned with captured Eldren treasure.

Begrudgingly the king had agreed to give Ermizhad decent quarters next to mine. His attitude towards me seemed to have changed since the first drunken night in Paphanaal. He was reserved, almost embarrassed by my presence. Doubtless he remembered vaguely that he had made some sort of fool of himself. Perhaps he resented my refusal to celebrate our victory; perhaps the glory that I had won for him made him jealous, though the gods knew I wanted nothing of that tainted glory.

Or perhaps he sensed my own disgust with the war I had agreed to fight for him and was nervous that I might suddenly refuse to be the champion he felt he so desperately needed?

I had no opportunity to discuss this with him and Count Roldero could offer no explanation save to say, in the king's favour, that the slaughter might have wearied Rigenos just as it had wearied me.

I was not sure of this, for Rigenos seemed to hate the Eldren even more than before, as was made evident by his treatment of Ermizhad.

Ermizhad still refused to speak. She hardly ate and she rarely left her cabin. But one evening, as I strolled on deck, I saw her standing at the rail and staring down into the sea as if she contemplated hurling herself into its depths.

I increased my pace so that I should be near if she did attempt to throw herself overboard. She half-turned as I approached and then looked away again.

At this point the king emerged on the poop deck and called down to me.

"I see you've taken pains to make sure the wind's behind you when you get near to the Eldren bitch, Lord Erekosë."

I stopped and looked up. At first, I hardly understood the reference. I glanced at Ermizhad, who pretended not to have heard the king's insult. I, too, pretended I had not understood the significance of the remark and gave a slight, polite bow.

Then, deliberately, I walked past Ermizhad and paused near the rail, staring out to sea.

"Perhaps you have no sense of smell, Lord Erekosë," the king called. Again I ignored the remark.

"It seems a pity that we must tolerate vermin on our ship when we took such pains to scrub our decks free of their tainted blood," the king went on.

At last, furious, I turned around, but he had left the poop deck. I looked at Ermizhad. She continued to stare into the dark waters as they were pierced by our oars. She seemed almost mesmerised by the rhythm. I wondered if she really had not heard the insults.

There were several more occasions of that kind on board the flagship *Iolinda* as we sailed for Noonos. Whenever King Rigenos got the opportunity, he would speak of Ermizhad in her presence as if she were not there; speak disdainfully of her and his disgust for all her kind.

Increasingly, I found it harder to control my anger, but control it I did, and Ermizhad, for her part, showed no sign that she was offended by the king's crude references to her and her race.

I saw less of Ermizhad than I wished but, in spite of the king's warnings, came to like her. She was certainly the most beautiful woman I had ever seen. Her beauty was different from the cool beauty of Iolinda, my betrothed.

What is love? Even now, now that the whole pattern of my particular destiny seems to have been fulfilled, I do not know. Oh, yes, I still loved Iolinda, but I think that, while I did not know it, I was falling in love with Ermizhad, too.

I refused to believe the stories told about her and esteemed her, though, at that time, I had no thought of letting this affect my attitude towards her. That attitude had to be of a gaoler for his prisoner—an important prisoner, at that. A prisoner who could help decide the war against the Eldren in our favour.

I did pause, once or twice, to wonder about the logic of keeping her as a hostage. If, as King Rigenos insisted, the Eldren were cold-hearted and unhuman, then why should Arjavh care that his sister would be murdered by us?

Ermizhad, if she were the creature King Rigenos believed her to be, showed no signs of her evil. Rather, she seemed to me to exhibit a singular nobility of soul that was in excellent contrast to the king's rude banter.

And then I wondered if the king realised the affection I felt for Ermizhad and was afraid that the union between his daughter and his immortal champion was threatened.

But I remained loyal to Iolinda. It did not occur to me to question that we should not be married on my return, as we had agreed.

There must be countless forms of love. Which is the form which conquers the rest? I cannot define it. I shall not try.

Ermizhad's beauty had the fascination of being an unhuman beauty, but close enough to my own race's ideal to attract me.

She had the long, pointed Eldren face that John Daker might have tried to describe as "elfin" and failed to do justice to its nobility. She had the slanting eyes that seemed blind in their strange milkiness, the slightly pointed ears, the high angular cheekbones and a slender body that was almost boyish. All the Eldren women were slender like this, small-breasted and narrow-waisted. Her red lips were fairly wide, curving naturally upwards so that she always seemed to be on the point of smiling when her face was in repose.

For the first two weeks of our voyage, she continued to refuse to speak, although I showed her elaborate courtesy. I saw that she had everything for her comfort and she thanked me through her guards, that was all. But one day I stood outside the set of cabins where she, the king and myself had our apartments, leaning over the rail and looking at a grey sea and an overcast sky, and I saw her approach me.

"Greetings, Sir Champion," she said half-mockingly as she came out of her cabin.

I was surprised.

"Greetings, Lady Ermizhad," said I. She was dressed in a cloak of midnight blue flung around a simple smock of pale blue wool.

"A day of omens, I think," she said, looking at the gloomy sky which boiled darkly now above us, full of heavy greys and dusty yellows.

"Why think you?" I enquired.

She laughed. It was lovely to hear—crystal and gold-strung harps. It was the music of heaven, not of hell. "Forgive me," she said. "I sought to disturb you—but I see you are not so prone to suggestion as others of your race."

I grinned. "You are very complimentary, my lady. I find their superstitions a trifle tedious, I must admit. As are their insults."

"One is not troubled by those," she said. "They are sad little insults, really."

"You are very charitable."

"We Eldren are a charitable race, I think."

"I have heard otherwise."

"I suppose you have."

"I have bruises that prove otherwise!" I smiled. "Your warriors did not seem particularly charitable in the sea-fight beyond Paphanaal."

She bowed her head. "And yours were not charitable when they came to Paphanaal. Is it true? Am I the only survivor?"

I licked my lips. They were suddenly dry. "I believe so," I said quietly.

"Then I am lucky," she said, her voice rising a little.

There was, of course, no reply I could make.

We stood there in silence, looking at the sea.

Later she said quietly: "So you are Erekosë. You are not like the rest of your race. In fact, you do not seem wholly of that race."

"Aha," I replied. "Now I know you are my enemy."

"What do you mean?"

"My enemies—the Lord Katorn in particular—suspect my Humanity."

"And are you human?"

"I am nothing else. I am sure of that. I have the uncertainties of any ordinary mortal. I am as confused as the rest, though my problems are, perhaps, different. How I came here, I do not know. They say I am a great hero reborn, come to aid them against your people. They brought me here by means of an incantation. But then it sometimes seems to me, in dreams, at night, that I have been many heroes."

"And all of them human?"

"I am not sure. I do not think my basic character has altered in any of those incarnations. I have no special wisdom, no special powers, so far as I know. Would you not think that an Immortal would have gathered a great store of wisdom?"

She nodded slightly. "I would think so, my lord."

"I am not even sure where I am," I continued. "I do not know if I came here from the far future or from the far past."

"The terms mean little to the Eldren," she said. "But some of us believe that past and future are the same—that Time moves in a circle, so that the past is the future and the future is the past."

"An interesting theory," I said. "But a rather simple one, is it not?"

"I think I would agree with you," she murmured. "Time is a subtle thing. Even our wisest philosophers do not fully understand its nature. The Eldren do not think very much about Time—we do not have to, normally. Of course, we have our histories. But history is not Time. History is merely a record of certain events."

"I understand you," I said.

Now she came and stood by the ship's rail, one hand resting lightly upon it.

At that moment I felt the affection that I suppose a father might have for a daughter, a father who delights in his offspring's assured innocence. She could not have been, I felt, much more than nineteen. Yet her voice had a confidence that comes with knowledge of the world, her carriage was proud, also confident. I realised then that Count Roldero might well have spoken the truth. How, indeed, could you gauge the age of an Immortal?

"I thought at first," I said, "that I came from your future. But now I am not sure. Perhaps I come from your past—that this world is, in relation to what I call the 'twentieth century', in the far future."

"This world is very ancient," she agreed.

"Is there a record of a time when only human beings occupied Earth?"

"We have no such records," she smiled. "There is an echo of a myth, the thread of a legend, which says that there was a time when only the Eldren occupied Earth. My brother has studied this. I believe he knows more."

I shivered. I did not know why, but my vitals seemed to chill within me. I could not, easily, continue the conversation, though I wanted to.

She appeared not to have noticed my discomfort.

At last I said: "A day of omens, madam. I hope to talk with you again soon." I bowed and returned to my cabin.

ᘑ 16 ᘒ

CONFRONTATION WITH THE KING

THAT NIGHT I slept without my usual precaution of a jug of wine to send me into deeper slumber. I did it deliberately, though with trepidation.

"EREKOSË..."

I heard the voice calling as it had called once before to John Daker. But this time it was not the voice of King Rigenos.

"Erekosë..."

This voice was more musical.

I saw green, swaying forests and great, green hills and glades and castles and delicate beasts whose names I did not know.

"Erekosë? My name is not Erekosë," I said. "It is Prince Corum. Prince Corum—Prince Corum Jhaelen Irsei in the Scarlet Robe— and I seek my people. O, where are my people? Why is there no cessation to this quest?"

I rode a horse. The horse was mantled in yellow velvet and hung about with panniers, two spears, a plain round shield, a bow and a quiver holding arrows. I wore a conical silver helm and a double weight of chainmail, the lower layer of brass and the upper of silver. And I bore a long, strong sword that was not the sword Kanajana.

"Erekosë."

"I am not Erekosë."

"Erekosë!"

"I am John Daker!"

"Erekosë!"

"I am Jerry Cornelius."

"Erekosë!"

"I am Konrad Arflane."

"Erekosë!"

"What do you want?" I asked.

"We want your help!"

"You have my help!"

"Erekosë!"

"I am Karl Glogauer!"

"Erekosë!"

"I seek lost Tanelorn."

The names did not matter. I knew it now. Only the fact mattered. The fact that I was a creature incapable of dying. A creature eternal. Doomed to have many shapes, to be called many names, but to be for ever battling.

And perhaps I had been wrong. Perhaps I was not truly human, but only assumed the characteristics of a human being if I were caught in a human body.

It seemed to me that I howled in misery then. What was I? What was I, if I were not a man?

The voice was still calling, but I refused to heed it. How I wished I had not heeded it before, as I lay in my comfortable bed, in the comfortable identity of John Daker.

* * *

I awoke and I was sweating. I had found out nothing more about myself and the mystery of my origin. It seemed I had only succeeded in confusing myself further.

It was still night, but I dared not fall asleep again.

I peered through the darkness. I looked at the curtains pulled across the windows, the white coverlet of the bed, my wife beside me.

I began to scream.

"EREKOSË—EREKOSË—EREKOSË."

"I am John Daker!" I screamed. "Look—I am John Daker!"

"EREKOSË."

"I know nothing of this name, Erekosë. My name is Elric, Prince of Melniboné. Elric Kinslayer. I am known by many names."

Many names—many names—many names…

How was it possible to possess dozens of identities all at the same time? To move from period to period at random? To move away from Earth itself, out to where the cold stars glared?

"I seek Tanelorn and peace. Oh, where lies Tanelorn?"

There was a rushing noise and then I plunged through dark, airless places, down, down, down. And there was nothing in the universe but drifting gas. No gravity, no colour, no air, no intelligence save my own—and perhaps, somewhere, one other.

Again I screamed.

And I refused to let myself know further.

Whatever the doom upon me, I thought next morning, I would never understand it. And it was probably for the best.

I went on deck and there was Ermizhad, standing in the same place at the rail, as if she had not moved all night. The sky had cleared somewhat and sunlight pushed thick beams through the clouds, the rays slanting down on the choppy sea so that the world was half-dark, half-light.

A moody day.

We stood for a while in silence, leaning out over the rail, watching the surf slide by, watching the oars smash into the waters in monotonous rhythm.

Again, she was the first to speak.

"What do they plan to do with me?" she asked quietly.

"You will be a hostage against the eventuality of your brother, Prince Arjavh, ever attacking Necranal," I told her. It was only half the truth. There were other ways of using her against her brother, but there was no point in detailing them. "You will be safe—King Rigenos will not be able to bargain if you are harmed."

She sighed.

"Why did not you and the other Eldren women flee when our fleets put in to Paphanaal?" I asked. This had puzzled me for some time.

"The Eldren do not flee," she said. "They do not flee from cities that they build themselves."

"They fled to the Mountains of Sorrow some centuries ago," I pointed out.

"No." She shook her head. "They were driven there. That is the difference."

"That is a difference," I agreed.

"Who speaks of difference?" A new, harsher voice broke in. It was King Rigenos. He had come silently out of his cabin and stood behind us, feet apart on the swaying deck. He did not acknowledge Ermizhad but stared directly at me. He did not look well.

"Greetings, sire," I said. "We were discussing the meaning of words."

"You've become uncommon friendly with the Eldren bitch!" he sneered. What was it about this man who had shown himself kind and brave in many ways that, when the Eldren were concerned, he became an uncouth barbarian?

"Sire," I said, for I could no longer be polite. "Sire, you speak of one who, though our enemy, is of noble blood."

Again he sneered. "Noble blood! The vile stuff which flows in their polluted veins cannot be termed thus! Beware, Erekosë! I realise that you are not altogether versed in our ways or our knowledge, that your memory is hazy—but remember that the Eldren wanton has a tongue of liquid gold which can beguile you to your doom and ours. Pay no heed to her!"

It was the most direct and most portentous speech he had made thus far.

"Sire," I said.

"She'll weave such a spell that you'll be a fawning dog at her mercy and no good to any of us. I tell you, Erekosë, beware. Gods! I've half a mind to give her to the rowers and let them have their way with her before she's thrown over the side!"

"You placed her under my protection, my lord king," I said angrily. "And I am sworn to protect her against all dangers!"

"Fool! I have warned you. I do not want to lose your friendship, Erekosë—and more, I do not want to lose our war champion. If she shows further signs of enchanting you, I shall slay her. None shall stop me!"

"I am doing your work, my king," I said, "at your request. But remember *you* this—I am Erekosë. I have been many other champions. What I do is for the human race. I have taken no oath of loyalty to you or to any other king. I am Erekosë, the War Champion, Champion of Humanity—not Rigenos's Champion!"

His eyes narrowed. "Is this treachery, Erekosë?" It was almost as if he hoped it were.

"No, King Rigenos. Disagreement with a single representative of Humanity does not constitute treachery to mankind."

He said nothing, but just stood there, seeming to hate me as much as he hated the Eldren girl. His breathing was heavy and rasped in his throat.

"Give me no reason to regret my summoning of thee, dead Erekosë," he said at length and turned away, going back into his cabin.

"I think it would be for the best if we discontinued our conversation," said Ermizhad quietly.

"Dead Erekosë, eh?" I said, and then grinned. "If I'm dead, then I'm strangely prone to emotion for a corpse." I made light of our dispute, yet events had taken a turn which caused me to fear that he would not, among other things, allow me the hand of Iolinda—for he still did not know that we were betrothed.

She looked at me strangely and moved her hand as if to comfort me.

"Perhaps I am dead," I said. "Have you seen any creatures like me on the Ghost Worlds?"

She shook her head. "Not really."

"So the Ghost Worlds do exist?" I said. "I had been speaking rhetorically."

"Of course they exist!" She laughed. "You are the greatest sceptic I have ever met!"

"Tell me about them, Ermizhad."

"What is there to tell?" She shook her head. "And if you do not believe what you have heard already, then there's little point if I tell you more that you will not believe, is there?"

I shrugged. "I suppose not." I felt she was being unduly secretive, but I did not press the matter.

"Answer one thing," I said. "Would the mystery of my existence be found on the Ghost Worlds?"

She smiled sympathetically. "How could I answer that, Erekosë?"

"I don't know. I thought the Eldren knew more of—of sorcery…"

"Now you are showing yourself to be as superstitious as your fellows," she said. "You do not believe…"

"Madam," I said, "I do not know what I should believe. The logic of this world—both human and Eldren—is, I fear, a mystery to me."

∾ 17 ∾

NECRANAL AGAIN

ALTHOUGH THE KING refrained from further outbursts against either myself or Ermizhad, it could not really be said that he warmed to me again, though he grew more relaxed as the shores of Necralala drew closer.

And eventually Noonos was sighted and we left the better part of the fleet there to refit and reprovision, and sailed back up the River Droonaa to come again to Necranal.

The news of our great sea victory was already in Necranal. Indeed, it had been amplified and it seemed that I had sunk some score of ships and destroyed their crews single-handedly!

I did nothing to deny the truth of this. I was worried King Rigenos would begin to work against me. The adulation of the people, however, meant that he could not be seen to deny me anything. My power had grown. I had achieved a victory, I had proved myself the champion the people wanted.

It now seemed that, if King Rigenos acted against me, he would arouse the wrath of the people against *him*—and that wrath would be so great it could lose him his crown—and his head.

This did not mean, of course, that he had to like me, but in fact, when we had once again reached the Palace of Ten Thousand Windows, he was almost in an affable mood.

Exhaustion makes us see threats from outside when really the threat is from within—the signals of failing physical powers: I think he had begun to see me as a threat to his throne, but the sight of his palace, his people and his daughter, the promise of rest and security, reassured him that he was still the king and would always be the king. I was not interested in his crown. I was interested only in his daughter.

Guards escorted Ermizhad away to her quarters when we arrived. She had departed before Iolinda came running down the stairs into the Great Hall, her face radiant, her carriage graceful, kissing first her father and then myself.

"Have you told Father of our secret?" she asked.

"I think he knew before we left." I laughed, turning to Rigenos, upon whose face there had come something of an abstracted look. "We would be betrothed, sire. Do you give us your consent?"

King Rigenos opened his mouth, wiped his forehead and swallowed before nodding. "Of course. My blessings to you. This will make our unity even stronger."

A slight frown came to Iolinda's brow. "Father—you are pleased, are you not?"

"Of c… yes, naturally I am pleased… naturally. But I am weary with travelling and with fighting, my dear. I need to rest. Forgive me."

"Oh, I am sorry, Father. Yes, you must rest. You do not look well. I will have the slaves prepare some food for you and you can dine in bed."

"Yes," he said, "yes."

* * *

When he had gone, Iolinda looked at me curiously. "You, too, seem to have suffered from the fighting, Erekosë. You are not hurt?"

"No. The battle was bloody. And I did not enjoy much of what we had to do."

"Warriors must kill. That is the way."

"But must they kill women, Iolinda? Must they kill children? Babies?"

She moistened her lips with her tongue. Then she said: "Come. Let's eat in my apartments. It is more restful there."

When we had eaten, I felt better, but was still not completely at ease.

"What happened?" she asked. "At Mernadin?"

"There was a great sea-fight. We won it."

"That is good."

"Yes."

"You took Paphanaal. You stormed it and took it."

"Who told you we 'stormed' it?" I asked in astonishment.

"Why, you do—the returning warriors. We heard the news shortly before you came back."

"The city gave no resistance," I told her. "There were some women in Paphanaal and there were some children in Paphanaal and they were butchered by our troops."

"A few women and children always get harmed in the storming of a city," said Iolinda. "You must not blame yourself if—"

"We did not storm the city," I repeated. "It was undefended. There were no men there. Every one of the male inhabitants of Paphanaal had sailed with the fleet we destroyed."

She shrugged. Evidently she could not visualise the true picture. Perhaps it was just as well. But I could not resist one further comment:

"And, although we would have won anyway, part of our sea victory was due to our treachery," I said.

"You were betrayed, did you say?" She looked up eagerly. "Some treachery of the Eldren?"

"The Eldren fought honourably. We slaughtered their commander during a truce."

"I see," she said. Then she smiled. "Well, we must help you forget such terrible things, Erekosë."

"I hope you can," I said.

The king announced our betrothal the next day and the news was received with joy by the citizens of Necranal. We stood before them on the great balcony overlooking the city. We smiled and waved but, when we went inside again, the king left us with a curt word and hurried away.

"Father really does seem to disapprove of our match," Iolinda said in puzzlement, "in spite of his consent."

"A disagreement about tactics while at war," I said. "You know how important we soldiers think these things. He will soon forget."

But I was perturbed. Here was I, a great hero, loved by the people, marrying the king's daughter as a hero should, and something was beginning to strike me as being not quite right. I had had the feeling for some time, but I could not trace the source. I did not know whether it was to do with my peculiar dreams, my worries concerning my origin or merely the crisis which seemed to be building between the king and myself. There again, I was still very weary and probably my anxiety was baseless.

Iolinda and I now went to the bridal bed together, as was the custom in the Human Kingdoms.

But, that first night, we did not make love.

* * *

Halfway through the night I felt my shoulder being touched and I straightened up almost instantly.

I smiled in relief.

"Oh, it is you, Iolinda."

"It is I, Erekosë. You moaned and groaned so in your sleep that I thought it better to wake you."

"Aye…" I rubbed my eyes. "I thank you." My memory was unclear, but it seemed to me that I had been experiencing the usual dreams.

"Tell me something of Ermizhad," Iolinda said suddenly.

"Ermizhad?" I yawned. "What of her?"

"You have seen much of her, I heard. You conversed with her. I have never conversed with an Eldren. Usually we do not take prisoners."

I smiled. "Well, I gather it's heresy to say so, but I found her quite—human."

"Oh, Erekosë. That's a joke in bad taste. They say she's beautiful. They say she has a thousand human lives to account for. She's evil, is she not? She has lured many men to their deaths."

"I did not ask her about that," I said. "Mainly we discussed broad matters of philosophy."

"She is very clever, then?"

"I do not know. She seemed almost innocent to me." Then I added hastily, diplomatically: "But perhaps that's her cleverness—to seem innocent."

Iolinda frowned. "Innocent! Ha!"

I was disturbed. "I only offer my impression, Iolinda. I have no opinions, really, concerning Ermizhad. Or for that matter the rest of the Eldren."

"Do you love me, Erekosë?"

"Of course."

"You would not betray me?"

I laughed and took her in my arms. "How could you fear such a thing?"

We fell again into sleep.

Next morning, King Rigenos, Count Roldero and myself got down to the serious business of planning our strategy. Concerning ourselves with maps and battle plans, the tensions between us began to relax. Rigenos was almost cheerful. We were in unison about what should be done. By now it was likely Prince Arjavh would be attempting to retake Paphanaal—and assuredly failing. Probably he would lay siege to it, but we could bring in supplies and weapons by ship, so he would waste his time. Meanwhile, our expedition to the Outer Islands would attack Eldren positions there and, Roldero and Rigenos assured me, make it impossible for them to call on their halfling allies.

The plan, of course, depended on Arjavh's attacking Paphanaal.

"But he would have been already on his way when we sailed in," Rigenos reasoned. "It would be pointless for him to turn back. What could he achieve by doing that?"

Roldero agreed. "I think it's pretty certain that he'll concentrate on Paphanaal," he said. "Another two or three days and our fleets will be ready to sail again. We'll soon have the Outer Islands subdued, then we move on to Loos Ptokai itself. With luck, Arjavh will still have his main force concentrated on Paphanaal. By the end of this year, every Eldren position will have fallen to us."

I was a trifle cynical about his overconfidence. Katorn at least would have been less sure. I half-wished, in fact, that Katorn was here. I respected his advice as a soldier and strategist.

Next day, while we still pored over maps, the news came.

It astonished us. It altered every plan we had made. It made nonsense of our strategy. It put us in a frightening position.

Arjavh, Prince of Mernadin, Ruler of the Eldren, had not attacked Paphanaal. A great proportion of our troops waited there to greet him, but he had not deigned to pay them a visit.

Perhaps he had never intended to march on Paphanaal.

Perhaps he had always planned to do what he had done now and it was we who were the dupes! We had been outmanoeuvred!

"I said that the Eldren were clever," said King Rigenos when we received the news. "I told you, Erekosë."

"I believe you now," I said softly, trying to grasp the enormity of what had happened.

"Now how do you feel about them, my friend?" Roldero said. "Are you still divided?"

I shook my head. My loyalties lay with Humanity. There was no time for conscience, no point in trying to understand these unhuman people. I had underestimated them and now it seemed that Humanity itself might have to pay the price.

Eldren ships had beached on the coasts of Necralala, on the eastern seaboard and reasonably close to Necranal. An Eldren army was pushing towards Necranal herself and, it was said, none could stand against it.

I cursed myself then. Rigenos, Katorn, Roldero, even Iolinda had all been right. I had been deceived by their golden tongues, their alien beauty.

And there was hardly a warrior in Necranal. Half our available force was in Paphanaal and it would take a month to bring them back. The fleet Eldren craft had probably crossed the ocean in half that time! We thought we had defeated their fleet at Paphanaal. We had only defeated a fraction of it!

There was fear on all our faces as we made hasty contingency plans.

"There's no point in recalling the troops in Paphanaal at this stage," I said. "By the time they got here, the battle would have been decided. Send a fast messenger there, Roldero. Tell them what has happened and let Katorn decide his own strategy. Tell him I trust him."

"Very well," Roldero nodded. "But our available warriors are scarce in number. We can get a few divisions from Zavara. There are troops at Stalaco, Calodemia and some at Dratarda. Perhaps they can reach us in a week. Then we have some men at Shilaal and Sinana, but I hesitate to recommend their withdrawal."

"I agree," I said. "The ports must be defended at all costs. Who knows how many other fleets the Eldren have?" I cursed. "If only we had some means of gathering intelligence. Some spies…"

"That's idle talk," Roldero said. "Who among our people could disguise himself as an Eldren? For that matter who would be able to stomach their company long enough?"

Rigenos said: "The only large force we have is at Noonos. We'll have to send for them and pray that Noonos is not attacked in their absence." He looked at me. "This is not your fault, Erekosë. We expected too much of you."

"Well," I promised him, "you can expect more of me now, King Rigenos. I'll drive the Eldren back."

Rigenos scowled thoughtfully. "There's one thing we have to bargain with," he said. "The Eldren bitch—Arjavh's sister."

And then an idea began to dawn on me. We had thought Prince Arjavh must certainly march on Paphanaal and he had not. We had never expected him to invade Necralala. But he had. Why?

"What of her?" I said.

"Could we not use her now? Tell Arjavh that, if he does not retreat, we will slay her?"

"Would he trust us?"

"That depends on how much he loves his sister, eh?" King Rigenos grinned, his spirits rising. "Yes. Try that, anyway, Erekosë. But do not go to him in weakness. Take all the divisions you can muster."

"Naturally," I said. "I have a feeling that Arjavh will not let sentiment stop him while there is a chance he can capture the capital."

King Rigenos ignored this. Even I wondered about the truth of it, particularly since I was beginning to think there might be something more to Arjavh's decision.

King Rigenos put his hand on my shoulder. "We have had our differences, Erekosë. But now we are united. Go. Do battle with the Hounds of Evil. Win the battle. Kill Arjavh. This is your opportunity to strike the head from the monster that is the Eldren. And if battle seems impossible—use his sister to buy time for us. Be brave, Erekosë, be cunning—be strong."

"I will try," I said. "I will leave at once to rally the warriors at Noonos. I'll take all available cavalry and leave a small force of infantry and artillery to defend the city."

"Do as you think fit, Erekosë."

I went back to our apartments and said farewell to Iolinda. She was full of sorrow.

I did not call on Ermizhad and tell her what we planned.

~∽ 18 ∽~

PRINCE ARJAVH

I RODE OUT in my proud armour at the head of my army. My lance flaunted my banner of a silver sword on a black field, my horse pranced, my stance was confident and I had five thousand knights at my back and no idea of the size of the Eldren army.

We rode from Noonos eastwards to where the Eldren were said to be marching. We planned to cut them off before they reached Necranal.

Well before we met Arjavh's forces, we heard stories of their progress from fleeing villagers and townspeople. Apparently the Eldren were marching doggedly for Necranal, avoiding any settlements they came to. There were no reports, so far, of Eldren atrocities. They seemed to be moving too fast to bother to waste time on civilians.

Arjavh appeared to have only one ambition—to reach Necranal in the shortest possible time. I knew little of the Eldren prince save that he was reputedly a monster incarnate, a slayer and torturer of women and children. I was impatient to meet him in battle.

And there was one other rumour concerning Prince Arjavh's army. They said it was partly comprised of halflings—creatures from the Ghost Worlds. This story had terrified my men, but I had tried to assure them that the rumours were false.

Roldero and Rigenos were not with me. Roldero had returned to supervise the defence of Necranal, should we be unsuccessful, and it was in Necranal that Rigenos also stayed.

For the first time now, I was on my own. I had no advisors. I felt I needed none.

The armies of the Eldren and the forces of Humanity saw each other at last when they reached a vast plateau known as the Plain of Olas, after an ancient city that had once stood there. The plateau was surrounded by the peaks of distant hills. It was green and the hills were purple and we saw the banners of the Eldren as the sun set and those banners shone as if they were flags of fire.

My marshals and captains were all for rushing upon the Eldren as soon as morning came. To our relief it seemed that their numbers were smaller than ours and it now looked likely we could defeat them.

I felt relieved. It meant that I did not need to use Ermizhad for bartering with Arjavh and I could afford to stand by the Code of War which the humans used among themselves but refused to extend to the Eldren.

My commanders were horrified when I told them, but I said: "Let us act well and with nobility. Let us set an example to them." Now there was no Katorn, no Rigenos—not even Roldero—to argue with me and tell me that we must be treacherous and quick where Eldren were concerned. I wanted to fight this battle in the terms that Erekosë understood, for I was following Erekosë's instincts now.

I watched our herald ride into the night under a flag of truce. I watched him ride away and then, on an impulse, spurred after him.

My marshals called after me: "Lord Erekosë—where do you go?"

"To the Eldren camp!" I called back, and laughed at their consternation.

The herald turned in his saddle, hearing the hoofbeats of my horse. "Lord Erekosë?" he said questioningly.

"Ride on, herald—and I'll ride with you."

And so, together, we came at last to the Eldren camp, and we stopped as the outer guards hailed us.

"What would you here, humans?" some low-ranking officer asked, peering with his blue-flecked eyes through the gloom.

The moon came out and shone silver. I took my banner from where it lay against my horse's side. I raised it and I shook it out. The moon picked up the motif.

"That is Erekosë's banner," said the officer.

"And I am Erekosë," I said.

A look of disgust crossed the Eldren's face. "We heard what you did at Paphanaal. If you were not here under the truce flag, I would…"

"I did nothing at Paphanaal I am ashamed of," I said.

"No. You would not be ashamed."

"My sword was sheathed during the whole stay at Paphanaal, Eldren."

"Aye—sheathed in the bodies of babes."

"Think what you will," I said. "Lead me to your master. I'll not waste time with you."

We rode through the silent camp until we came to the simple pavilion of Prince Arjavh. The officer went inside.

Then I heard a movement in the tent and from it stepped a lithe figure, dressed in half-armour, a steel breastplate strapped over a loose shirt of green, leather hose beneath leg greaves, also of steel, and sandals on his feet. His long black hair was kept away from his eyes by a band of gold bearing a single great ruby.

And his face—his face was beautiful. I hesitate to use the word to describe a man, but it is the only one that will do justice to those fine features. Like Ermizhad, he had the tapering skull, the slanting, orbless eyes. But his lips did not curve upwards as did hers. His mouth was grim and there were lines of weariness about it. He passed his hand across his face and looked up at us.

"I am Prince Arjavh of Mernadin," he said in his liquid voice. "What would you say to me, Erekosë, you who abducted my sister?"

"I came personally to bring the traditional challenge from the hosts of Humanity," I said.

He raised his head to look about him. "Some plot, I gather. Some fresh treachery?"

"I speak only the truth," I told him.

There was melancholy irony in his smile when he replied. "Very well, Lord Erekosë. On behalf of the Eldren, I accept your gracious challenge. We will battle, then, shall we? We will kill each other tomorrow, shall we?"

"You may decide when to begin," I said. "For it is we who made the challenge."

He frowned. "It has been perhaps a million years since the Eldren and Humanity fought according to the Code of War. How can I trust you, Erekosë? We have heard how you butchered the children."

"I butchered no children," I said quietly. "I begged that they be spared. But at Paphanaal I was advised by King Rigenos and his marshals. Now I control the battle forces and I choose to fight according to the Code of War. The Code of War, I believe, that I originally drew up."

"Aye," Arjavh said thoughtfully. "It's sometimes called Erekosë's Code. But you are not the true Erekosë. He was a mortal like all men. Only the Eldren are immortal."

"I am mortal in many respects," I said shortly, "and immortal in others. Now, shall we decide the terms of battle?"

Arjavh spread his arms. "Oh, how can I trust all this talk? How many times have we agreed to believe you humans and have been betrayed time after time? How can I accept that you are Erekosë, the Champion of Humanity, our ancient enemy whom, even in our legends, we respect as a noble foe? I wish to believe you, you who calls himself Erekosë, but I cannot afford to."

"May I dismount?" I asked. The herald glanced at me in astonishment.

"If you will."

I clambered from the back of my armoured horse and unbuckled my sword and hung it over the pommel of the saddle and I pushed the horse to one side and walked forward and stood there confronting Prince Arjavh face to face.

"We are a stronger force than you," I said. "We stand a good chance of winning the battle tomorrow. It is possible that within a week even the few who escape the battle will be dead at the hands of our soldiers or our peasants. I offer you the chance to fight a noble battle, Prince Arjavh. A fair battle. I suggest that the terms can include the sparing of prisoners, medical treatment for all captured wounded, a counting of the dead and of the living." I was remembering it all as I spoke.

"You know Erekosë's Code well," he said.

"I should."

He looked away and up at the moon. "Is my sister still alive?"

"She is."

"Why did you come thus with your herald to our camp?"

"Curiosity, I suppose," I told him. "I have spoken much with

Ermizhad. I wanted to see if you were the devil I heard you were—or the person Ermizhad described."

"And what do you see?"

"If you are a devil, you are a weary one."

"Not too weary to fight," he said. "Not too weary to take Necranal if I can."

"We expected you to march on Paphanaal," I told him. "We thought it logical that you would try to recapture your main port."

"Aye—that's what I planned. Then I learned that you had abducted my sister." He paused. "How is she?"

"Well," I said. "She was placed under my protection and I have seen to it that she has been treated with courtesy wherever possible."

He nodded.

"We come, of course, to rescue her," he said.

"I wondered if that was your reason." I smiled a little. "We should have expected it, but we did not. You realise that they will, should you win tomorrow's battle, threaten to kill her if you do not retreat."

Arjavh pursed his lips. "They will kill her, anyway, will they not? They will torture her. I know how they treat Eldren prisoners."

I could say nothing to the contrary.

"If they kill my sister," Prince Arjavh said, "I will burn down Necranal though I am the only one left to do it. I will kill Rigenos, his daughter, everyone."

"And so it goes on," I said softly.

Arjavh looked back at me. "I am sorry. You wished to discuss the terms of battle. Very well, Erekosë, I will trust you. I agree to all your proposals—and offer a term of my own."

"That is?"

"Deliverance of Ermizhad from captivity if we should win. It will save you and us many lives."

"It would," I agreed, "but it is not for me to make that bargain. I regret it, Prince Arjavh, but it is the king who holds her. If she were my prisoner and not just under my protection, I would do as you suggest. If you win, you must go on to Necranal and lay siege to the city."

He sighed. "Very well, Sir Champion. We shall be ready at dawn tomorrow."

I said hurriedly: "We outnumber you, Prince Arjavh. You could go back now—in peace."

He shook his head. "Let the battle be fought."

"Until dawn, then, Prince of the Eldren."

He moved his hand tiredly in assent. "Farewell, Lord Erekosë."

"Farewell." I mounted my horse and rode back to our camp in a sorrowful mood, the puzzled herald at my side.

Once again I was divided. Were the Eldren so clever they could deceive me so easily?

Tomorrow would tell.

That night in my own pavilion I slept as badly as ever, but I accepted the dreams, the vague memories, and I did not attempt to fight them, to interpret them. It had become clear to me that there was no point to it. I was what I was—I was the Eternal Champion, the Everlasting Wager of War. I would never know why.

Before dawn our trumpets warned us to awake and make ourselves ready. I buckled on my armour, my sword and my lance's cover was ripped off to reveal the long, metal-shod spear.

I went out into the chill of the dying night. The day was not yet with us. Silhouetted against what little light we had, my cavalry was already mounting. There was a cold, clammy sweat on my forehead. I wiped it with a rag time after time, but it remained there. I raised my helm and brought it down over my head, strapping it to my shoulder plates. My squires handed me my gauntlets and I pulled them on. Then, stiff-legged in my armour, I stalked towards my steed, was helped into the saddle, was handed my shield and my lance, and cantered up the line to the head of my troops.

It was very quiet when we began to move—a steel sea lapping at the coast that was the Eldren camp.

As the watery dawn broke, our forces sighted each other. The Eldren were still by their camp but, when they saw us, they too began to move. Very slowly, it seemed, but implacably.

I lifted my visor to get a wider view of the surroundings. The ground seemed good and dry. There appeared to be no places with superior advantages.

The horses' hoofs thumped the turf. The arms of the riders clattered at their sides. Their armour clashed and their harness creaked. But in spite of this a silence seemed to fill the air.

Nearer we came and nearer.

A flight of swallows flew high above us and then glided away towards the far-off hills.

I closed my visor. The back of the horse jogged beneath me. The cold sweat seemed to cover my body and clog my armour. The lance and the shield were suddenly very heavy.

I smelled the stink of other sweating men and horses. Before long, I would smell their blood, too.

Because of our need for speed, we had brought no cannon. The Eldren, also wishing to travel rapidly, had no artillery either.

Perhaps, I thought, their siege machines were following behind at a slower pace.

Nearer now. I could make out Arjavh's banner and a little cluster of flags that were those of his commanders.

I planned to depend upon my cavalry. They would spread out on two sides to surround the Eldren while another arrowhead of horsemen pierced the centre of their ranks and pushed through to the rear so that we would surround them on all sides.

Nearer still. My stomach grumbled and I tasted bile in my mouth.

Close. I reined in my horse and raised my lance and gave the order for the archers to shoot.

We had no crossbows, only longbows, which had greater range and penetrating power and could shoot many more arrows at a time. The first flight of arrows screamed overhead and thudded down into the Eldren ranks and then were almost instantly followed by another flight and then another.

Our shafts were answered by the slim arrows of the Eldren. Horses and men shrieked as the arrows found their marks and for a moment there was consternation among our men as their ranks became ragged. But then, with great discipline, they re-formed.

Again I raised my lance on which fluttered my black-and-silver pennant.

"Cavalry! Advance at full gallop!"

The trumpets shouted the order. The air was savaged by the sound. The knights spurred their war-steeds forward and began, line upon line of them, to fan out on two sides while another division rode straight towards the centre of the Eldren host. These knights were bent over the necks of their fast-moving horses, lances leaning at an angle across their saddles, some held under the right arm and aimed to the left and others secure under left arms, aimed at the right. Their helmet plumes fluttered behind them as they bore down on the Eldren. Their cloaks streamed out, and their pennants waved and the dim sunlight gleamed on their armour.

I was almost deafened by the thunder of hoofs as I kicked my charger into a gallop and, with a band of fifty picked knights behind me, they themselves surrounding the twin standards of Humanity, rode forward, straining my eyes for Arjavh whom, at that moment, I hated with a terrible hatred.

I hated him because I must fight this battle and possibly kill him.

With a fearful din made up of shouts and clashing metal, we smashed into the Eldren army and soon I was oblivious to all but the need to kill and defend my life against those who would kill me. I broke my lance early on. It smashed right through the armoured body of an Eldren noble and split with the impetus. I left it in him and drew my sword.

Now I hewed about me with savage intensity, seeking sight of Arjavh. At last I saw him, a huge mace swinging from his gauntleted hand, battering at the infantrymen who sought to pull him from his saddle.

"*Arjavh!*"

He glimpsed me from the corner of his eye as I waited for him. "A moment, Erekosë, I have work here."

"*Arjavh!*" The name I screamed was a challenge, nothing else.

Arjavh finished the last of the foot soldiers and he kicked his horse towards me, still flailing around him with his giant mace as two mounted knights came at him. Then the men drew back as they saw we were about to engage.

We came close enough to fight now. I aimed a mighty blow at him with my poisoned sword, but he pulled aside in time and I felt his mace glance off my back as I leaned so far forward in my saddle after the wasted blow that my sword almost touched the churned ground.

I brought the sword up in an underarm swing and the mace was there to deflect it. For several minutes we fought until, in my astonishment, I heard a voice some distance away.

"RALLY THE STANDARD! RALLY, KNIGHTS OF HUMANITY!"

We had not succeeded in our tactics! That was obvious from the cry. Our forces were attempting to consolidate and attack afresh. Arjavh smiled and lowered his mace.

"They sought to surround the halflings," he said and laughed aloud.

"We'll meet again soon, Arjavh," I shouted as I turned my horse back and spurred it through the press, forcing my way through the milling, embattled men towards the standard which swayed to my right.

There was no cowardice in my leaving and Arjavh knew it. I had to be with my men when they rallied. That was why Arjavh had lowered his weapon. He had not sought to stop me.

∽ 19 ∾

THE BATTLE DECIDED

ARJAVH HAD MENTIONED the halflings. I had noticed no ghouls amongst his men. What were they, then? What kind of creatures could not be surrounded?

The halflings were only part of my problem. Fresh tactics had to be decided upon hurriedly or the day would be soon lost. Four of my marshals were desperately trying to get our ranks re-formed as I came up to them. The Eldren enclosed us where we had planned to enclose them and many groups of our warriors were cut off from the main force.

Above the noise of the battle I shouted to one of my marshals: "What's the position? Why did we fail so quickly? We outnumber them."

"It's hard to tell what the position is, Lord Erekosë," the marshal answered, "or how we failed. One moment we had surrounded the Eldren and the next moment half their forces were surrounding us—they vanished and reappeared behind us! Even now we cannot tell which is material Eldren and which halfling." The man who answered me was Count Maybeda, an experienced old warrior. His voice was ragged and he was very much shaken.

"What other qualities do these halflings possess?" I asked.

"They are solid enough when fighting, Lord Erekosë, and they can be slain by ordinary weapons—but they can disappear at will and be wherever they wish on the field. It is impossible to plan tactics against such a foe."

"In that case," I decided, "we had best keep our men together and fight a defensive action. I think we still outnumber the Eldren and their ghostly allies. Let them come to us!"

The morale of my warriors was low. They were disconcerted and were finding it difficult to face the possibility of defeat when victory had seemed so certain.

Through the milling men I saw the basilisk banner of the Eldren approaching us. Their cavalry poured in swiftly with Prince Arjavh at their head.

Our forces came together again and once more I was doing battle with the Eldren leader.

He knew the power of my sword—knew that the touch of it could slay him if it fell on a break in his armour—but that deadly mace, wielded with the dexterity with which another would wield a sword, warded off every blow I aimed.

I fought him for half an hour until he showed signs of dazed weariness and my own muscles ached horribly.

And again our forces had been split! Again it was impossible to see how the battle went. For most of the time I was uncaring, oblivious to the events around me as I concentrated on breaking through Arjavh's splendid guard.

Then I saw Count Maybeda ride swiftly past me, his golden armour split, his face and arms bloody. In one red hand he carried the torn banner of Humanity and his eyes stared in fear from his wounded head.

"Flee, Lord Erekosë!" he screamed as he galloped past. "Flee! The day is lost!"

I could not believe it, until the ragged remnants of my warriors began to stream past me in ignominious flight.

"Rally, Humanity!" I called. "Rally!" But they paid me no heed. Again Arjavh dropped his mace to his side.

"You are defeated," he said.

Reluctantly I lowered my sword.

"You are a worthy foe, Prince Arjavh."

"You are a worthy foe, Erekosë. I remember our battle terms. Go in peace. Necranal will need you."

I shook my head slowly and drew a heavy breath. "Prepare to defend yourself, Prince Arjavh," I said.

He shrugged, swiftly brought up the mace against the blow I aimed at him and then brought it down suddenly upon my metal-gauntleted wrist. My whole arm went numb. I tried to cling to the sword, but my fingers would not respond. It dropped from my hand and hung by a thong from my wrist.

With a curse, I flung myself from my saddle straight at him, my good hand grasping at him, but he turned his horse aside and I fell, face forward, in the bloody mud of the field.

I attempted once to rise, failed and lost consciousness.

~20~

A BARGAIN

WHO AM I?
  You are Erekosë, the Eternal Champion.
WHAT IS MY REAL NAME?
  Whatever it happens to be.
WHY AM I AS I AM?
  Because that is what you have always been.
WHAT IS "ALWAYS"?
  Always.
WILL I EVER KNOW PEACE?
  You will sometimes know peace.
FOR HOW LONG?
  For a while.
WHERE DID I COME FROM?
  You have always been.
WHERE WILL I GO?
  Where you must.
FOR WHAT PURPOSE?
  To fight.
TO FIGHT FOR WHAT?
  To fight.

FOR WHAT?
Fight.
FOR WHAT?

I shivered, aware that I was no longer clad in my armour. I looked up. Arjavh stood over me.

"I wonder why he hated me then," he was murmuring to himself. Then he realised I was awake and his expression altered. He gave a light smile. "You're a ferocious one, Sir Champion."

I looked into his moody, milky eyes.

"My warriors," I said, "what…?"

"Those that were left have fled. We released the few prisoners we had and sent them after their comrades. Those were the terms, I believe?"

I struggled up. "Then you are going to release me?"

"I suppose so. Although…"

"Although?"

"You would be a useful bargaining prisoner."

I took his meaning and relaxed, sinking back onto the hard bed. I thought deeply and fought the idea which came to me. But it grew too large in me. At length I said, almost against my will: "Trade me for Ermizhad."

His cool eyes showed surprise for an instant. "You would suggest that? But Ermizhad is such a strong hostage for Humanity."

"Damn you, Eldren. I told you to trade me for her."

"You're a strange human, my friend. But with your permission granted, that is what I shall do. I thank you. You really do remember the old Code of War, don't you? I think you are who you say you are."

I closed my eyes. My head ached.

He left the tent and I heard him instructing a messenger.

"Make sure the people know!" I shouted from the bed. "The king may not agree, but the people will force his hand. I'm their hero! They'll willingly trade me for an Eldren—no matter who that Eldren is."

Arjavh instructed the messenger accordingly. He came back into the tent.

"It puzzles me," I said at length. He was sitting on a bench on the other side of the tent. "It puzzles me that the Eldren have not conquered Humanity before now. With those halfling warriors, I should think you'd be invincible."

He shook his head. "We rarely make use of our allies," he said. "But I was desperate. You can understand that I was prepared to go to almost any measures to rescue my sister."

"I can," I told him.

"We would never have invaded," he continued, "had it not been for her." It was said so simply that I believed him. I had already been fairly certain of that.

I took a deep breath. "It is hard for me," I said. "I am forced to fight like this, with no clear idea about the rights or the wrongs of that fighting, with no true knowledge of this world, with no opinions of those who inhabit it. Simple facts turn out to be lies—and unbelievable things turn out to be true. What are the halflings, for instance?"

Again he smiled. "Sorcerous ghouls," he said.

"That is what Count Roldero told me. It is no explanation."

"What if I told you they were capable of breaking up their atomic structure at will and assembling again in another place? You would not understand me. Sorcery, you would say."

I was surprised at the scientific nature of his explanation. "I would understand you better," I said slowly.

He raised his slanting eyebrows.

"You *are* different," he said. "Well, the halflings, as you have seen, are related to the Eldren. Not all the dwellers on the Ghost Worlds are our kin—some are more closely related to men, and there are other, baser forms of life.

"The Ghost Worlds are solid enough, but exist in an alternate series of dimensions to our own. There are many such series, our philosophers believe—possibly an infinite series. On the worlds we know, the halflings have no special powers—no more than we have—but here they have. We do not know why. They do not know why. On Earth different laws seem to apply for them. More than a million years ago we discovered a means of bridging the dimensions between Earth and these other worlds. We found a race akin to our own who will, at times, come to our aid if our need is especially great. This was one of those times. Sometimes, however, the bridge ceases to exist when the Ghost Worlds move into another phase of their weird orbit, so that any halflings on Earth cannot return and any of our people are in the same position if they are on the Ghost Worlds. Therefore, you will understand, it is dangerous to stay on either side overlong."

"Is it possible," I asked, "that the Eldren came originally from these Ghost Worlds?"

"I suppose it is possible," he agreed. "There are no records, though."

"Perhaps that is why the humans hate you as aliens," I suggested.

"That is not the reason," he told me, "for the Eldren occupied Earth for ages before humankind ever came here."

"What!"

"It is true," he said. "I am an immortal and my grandfather was an immortal. He was slain during the first wars between the Eldren and Humanity. When the humans came to Earth, they had incredible weapons of terrible destructive potential. In those days we also possessed similar weapons. The wars created such destruction that the Earth seemed like a blackened ball of mud when the wars were ended and the Eldren defeated. So terrifying was the destruction that we swore never again to use our weapons, whether we were threatened with extermination or not. We could not assume the responsibility for destroying an entire planet."

"You mean you still have these weapons?"

"They are locked away, yes."

"And you have the knowledge to use them?"

"Of course. We are immortal. We have many people who fought in those ancient wars, some even built new weapons before our decision was made."

"Then why...?"

"I have told you. We swore not to."

"What happened to the humans' weapons—and their knowledge of them? Did they make the same decision?"

"No. The human race degenerated. Wars occurred among themselves. At one time they almost wiped themselves out completely, at another they were barbarians, and at another they seemed to have matured, to have conquered their monstrous egos and found self-respect at last, to be at peace with their own souls and with one another. During one of those stages they lost the knowledge and the remaining weapons. In the last million years they have climbed back from absolute savagery—the peaceful years were short, a false lull—and I'd predict they'll sink back again soon enough. They seem bent on their own destruction as well as ours. We have wondered if the humans, who must surely exist in other planes, are the same. Perhaps not."

"I hope not," I said. "How do you think the Eldren will fare against the humans?"

"Badly," he said. "Particularly since the humans are inspired by your leadership and the gateway to the Ghost Worlds is due soon to close again. Previously Humanity was split by quarrels, you see. King Rigenos could never get his marshals to agree and he was too uncertain of himself to make the large decisions. But you have made decisions for him and you have united the marshals. You will win, I think."

"You are a fatalist," I said.

"I am a realist," he said.

"Could not peace terms be arranged?"

He shook his head. "What use is it to talk?" he asked me bitterly. "You humans, I pity you. Why will you always identify our motives with your own? We do not seek power—only peace. But that, I suppose, this planet shall never have until Humanity dies of old age."

I stayed with Arjavh for a few more days before he released me, on trust, and I rode back towards Necranal. It was a long, lonely ride and I had a great deal of time to think.

I was hardly recognised this time, for I was dusty and my armour was battered and the people of Necranal had become used to seeing beaten warriors returning to the city.

I reached the Palace of Ten Thousand Windows. A gloomy quiet had settled on it. The king was not in the Great Hall and Iolinda was not in her quarters.

In my old apartments, I stripped off my armour. "When did the Lady Ermizhad leave?" I asked a slave.

"Leave, master? Is she not still here?"

"What? Where?"

"In the same quarters, surely."

I still had my breastplate on and I donned my sword as I strode through the corridors until I got to Ermizhad's apartments and brushed past the guard on the door.

"Ermizhad—you were to be traded for me. Those were the terms. Where is the king? Why has he not kept his word?"

"I knew nothing of this," she said. "I did not know Arjavh was so close, otherwise…"

I interrupted her. "Come with me. We'll find the king and get you on your journey back."

I half dragged her from room to room of the palace until at last I found the king in his private apartments. He was in conference with Roldero as I burst in upon them.

"King Rigenos, what is the meaning of this? My word was given to Prince Arjavh that Ermizhad was to leave here freely upon my release. He allowed me to leave his camp on trust and now I return to find the Lady Ermizhad still in captivity. I demand that she be released immediately."

The king and Roldero laughed at me.

"Come now, Erekosë," said Roldero. "Who needs to keep his word to an Eldren jackal? Now we have our war champion back and still retain our chief hostage. Forget it, Erekosë. There is no need to regard the Eldren as human!"

Ermizhad smiled. "Do not worry, Erekosë. I have other friends." She closed her eyes and began to croon. At first the words came softly, but the volume rose until she was giving voice to a weird series of harmonies.

Roldero jumped forward, dragging out his sword.

"Sorcery!"

I stepped between them.

Roldero said urgently: "Erekosë! The bitch invokes her demon kind!"

I drew my own sword and held it warningly in front of me, protecting Ermizhad. I had no idea what she was doing, but I was going to give her the chance, now, to do whatever she wanted.

Her voice changed abruptly and then stopped. Then she cried: "Brethren! Brethren of the Ghost Worlds—aid me!"

⤳ 21 ⤲

AN OATH

QUITE SUDDENLY THERE materialised in the chamber some dozen or so Eldren, their faces but slightly different from others I had seen. I recognised them now as halflings.

"There!" shouted Rigenos. "Evil sorcery. She is a witch. I told you! A witch!"

The halflings were silent. They surrounded Ermizhad until all their bodies touched hers and one another's. Then Ermizhad shouted: "Away, brethren—back to the camp of the Eldren!"

Their forms began to flicker so that they seemed half in our dimension, half in some other. "Goodbye, Erekosë," she cried. "I hope we shall meet in happier circumstances."

"I hope so!" I shouted back. And then she vanished.

"Traitor!" cursed King Rigenos. "You aided her escape!"

"You should die by torture!" added Roldero, disgusted.

"I'm no traitor, as well you know," I said evenly. "You are traitors—traitors to your words, to the great tradition of your ancestors. You have no case against me, you stupid—stupid brutes."

I stopped, turned on my heel and left the chamber.

"You lost the battle—War Champion!" screamed King Rigenos after me as I stalked out. "The people do not respect defeat!"

I went to find Iolinda.

She had been walking in the balconies and had now returned to her apartments. I kissed her, needing at that moment a woman's friendly sympathy, but I seemed to meet a block. She was not, it seemed, prepared to give me help, although she kissed me dutifully. At length I ceased to embrace her and stood back a little, looking into her eyes.

"What's wrong?"

"Nothing," she said. "Should there be? You are safe. I had feared you dead."

Was it me, then? Was it? I pushed the thought from me. But can a man force himself to love a woman? Can he love two women at the same time? I was desperately clinging to the strands of the love I had felt for her when first we met.

"Ermizhad is safe," I blurted. "She called her halfling brothers to her aid and, when she returns to the Eldren camp, Arjavh will take his forces back to Mernadin. You should be pleased."

"I am," she said, and then: "And you are pleased, no doubt, that our hostage escaped!"

"What do you mean?"

"My father told me how you'd been enchanted by her wanton sorcery. You seemed to be more anxious for her safety than ours."

"That is foolish talk."

"You seem to like the company of the Eldren, too. Holidaying with our greatest enemy…"

"Stop!"

"I think my father spoke true, Erekosë." Her voice was subdued now. She turned from me.

"But, Iolinda, I love you. You alone."

"I do not believe you, Erekosë."

What is it in me that I should become what I became then? At that moment I gave an oath which was to affect all our destinies.

Why, as my love for her began to fade and I saw her as a selfish, grasping fool, did I yet protest a greater love for her?

I do not know. I only know that I did it.

"I love you more than life, Iolinda!" I said. "I would do anything for you!"

"I do not believe you!"

"I do. I will prove it!" I cried in agony.

She turned. There was pain and reproach in her eyes. There was a bitterness that went so deep it had no bottom. There was anger and there was revenge.

"How will you prove it, Erekosë?" she said softly.

"I swear I shall kill all the Eldren."

"All?"

"Every single Eldren."

"You will spare none?"

"None! None! I want it to be over. And the only way I can finish it is to kill them all. Then it will be over—only then!"

"Including Prince Arjavh and his sister?"

"Including them!"

"You swear this? You swear it?"

"I swear it. And when the last Eldren dies, when the whole world is ours, then I will bring it to you and we shall be married."

She nodded. "Very well, Erekosë." She went swiftly from the room.

I unstrapped my sword and flung it savagely to the floor. I spent the next few hours fighting my own agony of spirit.

But I had made the oath now.

Soon I became cold. I meant what I had said. I would destroy all the Eldren. Rid the world of them. Rid myself of this continual turmoil in my mind.

∾22∾

THE REAVING

THE LESS OF a man I became, and the more of an automaton, so the dreams and half-memories ceased to plague me. It was as if they had deliberately driven me into this mindless rôle; so long as I continued to be a creature without remorse or conscience they would reward me with their absence. If I again showed signs of ordinary Humanity, then they would punish me with their presence.

But that is a notion. It is no nearer the truth, I suppose, than any other. One might also argue that I was about to achieve the catharsis that would rid me of any ambivalence; banish my nightmares; cleanse my psyche.

In the month I spent preparing for the great war against the Eldren, I saw but little of my betrothed and, finally, ceased to seek her out, concentrating instead on the plans for the campaigns we intended to fight.

I developed the strictly controlled mind of the soldier. I allowed no emotion, whether it was love or hate, to influence me.

I became strong. And in my strength I became virtually inhuman. I knew people remarked upon it—but they also saw in me the qualities of a great battle leader and, while all avoided my company socially, they were very glad that Erekosë led them.

* * *

Arjavh and his sister returned to their ships and in their ships went back to their own land. Now, doubtless, they awaited us, readying themselves for the next battle.

We continued with our original plans and at length were ready to sail for the Outer Islands at World's Edge. The gateway to the Ghost Worlds which we intended to close.

Then we sailed.

It was a long and arduous sailing, that one, before we sighted the bleak cliffs of the Outer Islands and prepared ourselves for the invasion.

Roldero was with me. But it was a grim Roldero, a silent Roldero who had made himself, as I had, into nothing but an instrument of war.

Warily we sailed in. The Eldren, however, had known of our coming and had all but deserted their towns. This time there were no women and no children, nought but a few handfuls of Eldren warriors whom we slew. And of halflings there were none. Arjavh had spoken the truth when he said the gates were closing to the Ghost Worlds.

We ripped the towns to rubble, burning and pillaging as a matter of course, but without lust. We tortured captured Eldren to discover the meaning for this desertion and they told us nothing intelligible; but secretly I knew the meaning. Our troops became morose, possessed of a sense of anticlimax and, though we left no building standing, no Eldren alive, the men could not rid themselves of the notion that they had been thwarted in some inexplicable way—as an ardent lover is innocently thwarted by a coy maiden.

And, because of the Eldren's refusal to give them a mighty battle, our soldiers grew to hate the Eldren that much more.

* * *

When our work was done in the Outer Islands, and every building was dust, every Eldren a corpse, we sailed almost immediately for the continent of Mernadin and put into Paphanaal, which was still held by our forces under the Lord Katorn. But, in the meantime, King Rigenos had joined them and was waiting for us to arrive. We landed our troops and pushed outwards across the continent, bent on conquest.

I remember few incidents in detail. Days merged one into the other and wherever we went we slew Eldren. There was no Eldren fortress which could withstand our grim thrusting.

I was tireless in my murdering; insatiable in my bloodlust. Humanity had wanted such a wolf as I, and now they had him and they followed him, and they feared him.

It was a year of fire and steel and ruined flesh; Mernadin seemed at times to be nothing but a sea of smoke and blood. The troops were all physically weary, but the spirit of slaughter was in them and it gave them a horrible vitality.

A year of pain and death. Everywhere that the banners of Humanity met the standards of the Eldren, the basilisk standards would be torn down and trampled.

We put all we found to the sword. We mercilessly punished deserters in our own ranks, we flogged our troops to greater endurance.

We were the horsemen of death, King Rigenos, Lord Katorn, Count Roldero and myself. We grew as gaunt as hungry dogs and it seemed we fed on Eldren flesh, drank only Eldren blood. Fierce dogs we were. Wild-eyed and panting dogs, sharp-fanged dogs for ever restless for the scent of fear and death.

Towns burned behind us, cities fell and were crushed, stone by stone, to the ground. Eldren corpses littered the countryside and the fairest of our camp followers were fat carrion birds and sleek-coated jackals. A year of bloodshed. A year of destruction. But was it Mernadin I wished to destroy, or was it myself? If I could not force myself to love, then I could force myself to hate; and this I did. All feared me, humans and Eldren alike, as I turned beautiful Mernadin into a funeral pyre on which I sought, in terrible bewilderment and grief, to burn the decaying vestiges of my own Humanity.

I cannot justify my actions. Roldero had said that men must be judged by their deeds, not their motives. I offer such speculation only in the hope that by understanding our motives we may thus control our deeds.

It was in the Valley of Kalaquita, where stood the garden city of Lakh, that King Rigenos was killed.

The city looked peaceful and deserted, and we rode down upon it with little caution. We howled one great, concerted war-cry and, in place of the disciplined army which had landed at Paphanaal, we were one mass of blood-encrusted armour and dust-ingrained flesh, waving our weapons and galloping wildly upon that garden city of Lakh.

It was a trap.

The Eldren were in the hills and had used their beautiful city as bait. Silver-snouted cannon suddenly shouted from surrounding copses and sent a searing shower of shot into our astonished soldiers' midst! Slender arrows whistled in a wave of sharp-tipped terror as the hidden Eldren archers took their vengeance with their bows.

Horses fell. Men screamed. We turned in confusion. But then our own bowmen began to retaliate, concentrating not on the enemy archers, but on their cannoneers. Gradually the silver guns went silent and the archers melted back into the hills, retreating again to one of their few remaining fortresses.

I turned to King Rigenos, who sat beside me on his big war-steed. He was rigid, staring up at the sky. And then I saw that an arrow had pierced his thigh and embedded itself in his saddle, pinning him to his horse.

"Roldero!" I shouted. "Get a doctor for the king if we have one."

Roldero rode up from where he had been taking account of our dead. He pushed back the king's visor and shrugged. Then he stared significantly at me. "He has not breathed for several minutes by the look of him."

"Nonsense. An arrow in the thigh doesn't kill. Not normally, at any rate—and not so quickly. Get the doctor."

A peculiar smile crossed Roldero's bleak features. "It was the shock, I think, that killed him." Then he laughed brutally and pushed at the armoured corpse with his hand so that it tilted over, wrenching the arrow free, and crashed into the mud. "Your betrothed is queen now, Erekosë," said Roldero, still laughing. "I congratulate you."

My horse stirred as I stared down at Rigenos's corpse. Then I shrugged and turned my steed away.

It was our habit with the dead to leave them, no matter who they had been, where they lay.

We took Rigenos's horse with us. It was a good horse.

The loss of the king did not worry our warriors much, though Katorn himself seemed a little perturbed, perhaps because he had had such great influence over the monarch. But the king had possessed no real authority in this last year, for Humanity followed a grimmer chief, who some thought might be Death Himself.

Dead Erekosë is what they called me. The vengeful, mindless Sword of Humanity.

I did not care what they called me—Reaver, Bloodletter, Berserker—for my dreams no longer plagued me, my own hypocrisy did not disturb me, and my ultimate goal came closer and closer.

It was the last fortress of the Eldren left undefeated. I dragged my armies behind me as if by a rope. I dragged them towards the principal city of Mernadin, by the Plains of Melting Ice, Arjavh's capital—Loos Ptokai.

And at last we saw its looming towers silhouetted against a red evening sky. Of marble and black granite, it rose mighty and seemingly invulnerable above us."

But I knew we should take it.

I had Arjavh's word for it, after all. He had told me we should win.

The night after we had camped beneath the walls of Loos Ptokai, I sprawled in my chair and could not sleep. Instead I stared into the darkness. This was not my habit. Normally I would now slump into my bed and snore till dawn, wearied by the day's killing.

But tonight I brooded.

And then, at dawn the next day, my features cold as stone, I rode beneath my banner as I had ridden a year before into the camp of the Eldren, with my herald at my side.

We came close to the main gate of Loos Ptokai and then we stopped. A few Eldren looked down from distant battlements but I could not read their expressions.

My herald raised his golden trumpet to his lips and blew an eery blast upon it which echoed among the black and white towers of Loos Ptokai.

"Eldren prince!" I called in my dead voice. "Arjavh of Mernadin, I have come to slay you."

Then on the battlements directly over the great main gate I saw Arjavh appear. He peered down at me and there was a sadness in his strange eyes.

"Greetings, old enemy," he called. "You will have a long siege before you break this, the last of our strength."

"So be it," I said, "but break it we shall."

Arjavh paused. Then he said: "We once agreed to fight a battle according to the Erekosian Code of War. Do you wish to discuss terms again?"

I shook my head. "We shall not stop until every Eldren is slain. I have sworn an oath, you see, to rid Earth of all your kind."

"Then," said Arjavh, "before the battle commences, I invite you to enter Loos Ptokai as my guest and refresh yourself. You would seem in need of refreshment."

At this I bridled, but then my herald sneered. "They become ingenuous in their defeat, master, if they think they can deceive you by such a simple trick."

My mind had once again suddenly become a battleground of conflicting emotions. "Be silent!" I ordered the herald. I took a deep breath.

"Well?" called Arjavh.

"I accept," I said hollowly. And then I added: "Is the Lady Ermizhad therein?"

"She is—and is eager to see you again." There was an edge to Arjavh's voice as he answered this last question. For a moment I was again suspicious; did I detect the threat of treachery?

Arjavh must have been aware of my own affection for his sister: the affection I did not admit, but which secretly contributed to my decision to enter Loos Ptokai.

The herald said in astonishment: "My lord, surely you cannot be serious? As soon as you are inside the gates, you will be slain. There were stories once that you and Prince Arjavh were on not unfriendly terms, for enemies, but after the havoc you have caused in Mernadin, he will kill you immediately. Who would not?"

I shook my head. I was in a new and quieter mood. "He will not," I said. "And this way I can find an opportunity to judge the Eldren strength. It will be useful to us."

"But disastrous for us, if you should die."

"I will not die," I said, and then, incredibly, all the ferocity, the hate, the mad battle-anger, rushed out of me, leaving me, as I turned away from the herald so he should not see, with tears in my eyes.

"Open your gates, Prince Arjavh," I called in shaking tones. "I come to Loos Ptokai as your guest."

~23~

IN LOOS PTOKAI

I RODE MY horse slowly into the city, having left my sword and lance with the herald, who was now, in astonishment, galloping back to our own camp to give the news to the marshals.

The streets of Loos Ptokai were silent, as if in mourning. And when Arjavh came down the steps from the battlements to greet me, I saw, that he, too, wore the expression which showed upon my own harsh features. His step was not so lithe and his voice not quite so lilting as when we had first met a year before.

I dismounted. He gripped my arm.

"So," he said in attempted gaiety, "the barbarian battlemonger is still material. My people had begun to doubt it."

"I suppose they hate me," I said.

He seemed a little surprised. "The Eldren cannot hate," he said as he led me towards his palace.

I was shown by Arjavh to a small room containing a bed, a table and a chair of wonderful workmanship, all slender and seemingly of precious metal but in fact of cunningly wrought wood. In one corner was a sunken bath with water steaming in it.

When Arjavh had gone, I stripped off my blood- and dust-encrusted armour and climbed out of the underclothes I had worn for much of the past year. Then I sank gratefully into the water.

Since the initial emotional shock I had received when Arjavh had issued his invitation, my mind had become numbed. But now, for the first time in a year, I relaxed, mentally and physically, washing all the grief and hatred from me as I washed my body. So suddenly did the tension leave me that it might have been the result of Eldren sorcery; but I think now that I relaxed because I did not have to deceive myself in Loos Ptokai.

I was almost cheerful as I donned the fresh clothes which had been laid out for me and, when someone knocked at my door, called lightly for them to enter.

"Greetings, Erekosë." It was Ermizhad.

"My lady." I bowed.

"How are you faring, Erekosë?"

"In war, as you know, I am faring well. And personally I feel better for your hospitality."

"Arjavh sent me to bring you to the meal."

"I am ready. But first tell me how you have fared, Ermizhad."

"Well enough—in health," said she. Then she came closer to me. Involuntarily I leaned back slightly. She looked at the ground and raised her hands to touch her throat. "And tell me—are you now wed to Queen Iolinda?"

"We are still betrothed," I told her.

Deliberately, then, I looked into Ermizhad's eyes and added as levelly as I could: "We are to be married when…"

"When?"

"When Loos Ptokai is taken."

She said nothing.

I stepped forward so that we were separated by little more

than an inch. "Those are the only terms on which she will accept me," I said. "I must destroy all the Eldren. Your trampled banners will be my wedding gift to her."

Ermizhad nodded and gave me a queer, sad and sardonic look. "That is the oath you swore. You must abide by it. You must slay every Eldren. Every one."

I cleared my throat. "That is the oath."

"Come," she said. "The meal grows cold."

At dinner, Ermizhad and I sat close together and Arjavh spoke wittily of some of the stranger experiments of his scientist ancestors and for a little while we managed to drive away the knowledge of the forthcoming battle. But later, as Ermizhad and I talked softly to one another, I caught a look of pain in Arjavh's eyes and for a moment he was quiet. He broke into our conversation suddenly:

"We are beaten, as you know, Erekosë."

I did not want to speak of these things any more. I shrugged and tried to continue the lighter talk with Ermizhad. But Arjavh was insistent.

"We are doomed, Erekosë, to fall beneath the swords of your great army."

I drew a deep breath and looked him full in the face. "Yes. You are doomed, Prince Arjavh."

"It is a matter of time before you raze our Loos Ptokai."

This time I avoided his urgent gaze and merely nodded.

"So—you..." He broke off.

I became impatient. Many emotions mingled in me. "My oath," I reminded him. "I must do what I swore I would do, Arjavh."

"I do not fear to lose my own life..." he began.

"I know what you fear," I told him.

"Could not the Eldren admit defeat, Erekosë? Could they not acknowledge mankind's victory? Surely, one city…?"

"I swore an oath." Now sadness filled me.

"But you cannot…" Ermizhad gestured with her slim hand. "We are your friends, Erekosë. We enjoy each other's company. We—we *are* friends."

"We are of different races," I said. "We are at war."

"I am not asking for mercy," Arjavh said.

"I know that," I replied. "I do not doubt Eldren courage. I have seen too many examples of it."

"You abide by an oath given in anger, offered to an abstraction, that leads you to slay those you love and respect. An oath made to strengthen an already faltering resolve. You hated killing. I know you did!" Ermizhad's voice was puzzled. "Are you tired of killing, Erekosë?"

"I am very tired of killing," I told her.

"Then…?"

"But I began this thing," I continued. "Sometimes I wonder if I really do lead my men—or if they push me ahead of them. Perhaps I am wholly their creation. The creation of the will of Humanity. Perhaps I am a kind of patchwork hero that they have manufactured. Perhaps I have no other existence and when my work is done, I will fade as their sense of danger fades."

"I think not," said Arjavh soberly.

I shrugged. "You are not me. You have not had my strange dreams."

"You still have those dreams?" Ermizhad asked.

"Not recently. Since I began this campaign, they have gone away. They only plague me when I attempt to assert my own individuality. When I do what is required of me, they leave me in peace. I am a ghost, you see. Nothing more."

Arjavh sighed. "I do not understand this. I think you are suffering from a terrible self-deception, Erekosë. You could assert your own will—but you are *afraid* to! Instead, you abandon yourself to hate and bloodshed, to this peculiar melancholia of yours. You are depressed because you are *not* doing what you really desire to do. The dreams will come again, Erekosë. Mark my words—the dreams will come again and they will be more terrible than any you have experienced before."

"Stop!" I shouted. "Do not spoil this last meeting of ours. I came here because…"

"Because?" Arjavh raised a slim eyebrow.

"Because I needed some civilised company."

"To see your own kind," Ermizhad said softly.

I turned on her, rising from the table. "You are not my own kind! My race is out there, beyond those walls, waiting to vanquish you!"

"We are kin in spirit," Arjavh said. "Our bonds are finer and stronger than bonds of blood."

My face twisted and I buried it in my hands. "No!"

Arjavh put a hand on my shoulder. "You are more substantial than you will allow yourself to be, Erekosë. It would take a great deal of a particular kind of courage if you would pursue the implications of another course of action."

I let my hands fall to myself. "You are right," I told him. "And I do not have that courage. I am just a sword. A force, like a whirlwind. There is nothing else to me—nothing I would allow. Nothing I am allowed…"

Ermizhad interrupted fiercely. "For your own sake, you must allow that other self to rule. Forget your oath to Iolinda. You do not love her. You have nothing in common with the bloodthirsty rabble that follows you. You are a greater man than any you lead—greater than any you fight."

"Stop it! This is Eldren sophistry. You would save your skins with words, having failed with swords!"

"She is right, Erekosë," Arjavh said. "It is not for *our* lives that we argue. It is for *your* spirit."

I slumped down into my seat. "I sought to avoid confusion," I said, "by taking a simple course of action. It is true that I feel no kinship with those I lead—or those who thrust me before them—but undeniably they *are* my kin. My duty…"

"Let them fare how they will," Ermizhad said. "Your duty is not to them. It is to yourself."

I sipped some wine. Then I said quietly: "I am afraid."

Arjavh shook his head. "You are brave. It is not your fault."

"Who knows?" I said. "Perhaps at some stage in one of my incarnations I committed an enormous crime. And now I am paying the price."

"That is self-pitying speculation," Arjavh reminded me. "It is not—it is not—manly, Erekosë."

I inhaled deeply. "I suppose not." Then I looked at him. "But if Time is cyclic—in some form, at least—it could be that I have not yet committed that crime."

"It is idle to speak of 'crime' in this way," Ermizhad said impatiently. "What does your heart tell you to do?"

"My heart? I have not listened to it for many months."

"Listen to it now!" she said.

I shook my head. "I have forgotten how to listen to it, Ermizhad. I must finish what I set out to do. What I was called here to do."

"Are you sure it was King Rigenos who called you?"

"Who else?"

Arjavh smiled. "This, too, is idle speculation. You must do what you must do, Erekosë. I will plead for my people no longer."

"Thank you for that," I said. I rose, staggered slightly and screwed up my eyes. "Gods! I am so *weary*!"

"Rest here tonight," Ermizhad said quietly. "Rest with me."

I looked at her.

"With me," she said.

Arjavh began to speak, changed his mind and left the room.

I realised then that I wanted nothing else but to do as Ermizhad suggested. Yet I shook my head. "It would be weakness."

"No," she said. "It would give you strength. It would enable you to make a clearer decision."

"I have made my decision. Besides, my oath to Iolinda…"

"You swore no oath of faithfulness."

I spread my hands. "I cannot remember."

She moved towards me and stroked my face. "Perhaps it would end something," she suggested. "Perhaps it would restore your love for Iolinda."

Now physical pain seemed to seize me. I even wondered for a moment if they had poisoned me. "No."

"It would help," she said. "I know it would help. How, I am not sure. I do not even know if it suits my own desires, but…"

"I *cannot* weaken now, Ermizhad."

"Erekosë, it would *not* be weakness!"

"Still…"

She turned away from me and said in a soft, strange tone, "Then rest here anyway. Sleep in a good bed so that you will be fit for tomorrow's fighting. I love you, Erekosë. I love you more than I love anything. I will aid you in whatever course of action you decide upon."

"I have already decided," I reminded her. "And you cannot aid me there." I felt dizzy. I did not want to return to my own camp in that condition, for they would be sure I had been drugged and would lose all confidence in me. Better to stay the night and greet my troops refreshed. "Very well, I will stay here tonight," I said. "Alone."

"As you wish, Erekosë." She moved towards the door. "A servant will come to show you where to sleep."

"I'll sleep in this room," I told her. "Have someone bring in a bed."

"As you wish."

"It will be good to sleep in a real bed," I said. "My thoughts will be sharper in the morning."

"I hope so. Goodnight, Erekosë."

Had they known that the dreams would return that night? Was I the victim of immense and subtle cunning such as only the unhuman Eldren possessed?

I lay on my bed in the Eldren fortress city and I dreamed.

But this was not a dream in which I sought to discover my true name. I had no name in this dream. I did not want a name.

I watched the world turning and I saw its inhabitants running about its surface like ants in a hill, like beetles in a dungheap. I saw them fighting and destroying, making peace and building— only to drag those buildings down again in another inevitable war. And it seemed to me that these creatures had evolved only so far from the beast state and that some quirk of destiny had doomed them to repeat, over and over again, the same mistakes. And I realised that there was no hope for them—these imperfect creatures that were halfway from the animals, halfway from the gods—that it was their fate, like mine, to struggle for ever and forever fail to be fulfilled. The paradoxes that existed in me existed in the whole race. The problems for which I could find no solution in fact had no solution. There was no point in seeking an answer; one could only accept what existed or else reject it, as one pleased. It would always be the same. Oh, there was much to love them for and nothing at all to hate them for. How could they be hated, when their errors resulted from the quirk of fate that had made them the half-creatures that they were—half-blind, half-deaf, half-dumb...

I woke up and felt very calm. And then, gradually, a sense of terror possessed me as the implications of my thoughts began to dawn on me.

Had the Eldren sent this dream—with their sorcery?

I did not think so. This dream was the dream that the other dreams had sought to hide from me. I was sure of it. This was the stark truth.

And the stark truth horrified me.

It was not my fate to wage eternal war—it was the fate of my entire race. As part of that race—as its representative, in fact—I, too, must wage eternal war.

And that is what I wished to avoid. I could not bear the thought of fighting for ever, wherever I was required. And yet whatever I did to try to end the cycle would be hopeless. There was only one thing I could do.

I buried the thought.

But what else?

Try for peace? See if it would work? Let the Eldren live?

Arjavh had expressed impatience with idle speculation. But this, too, was idle speculation. The human race was sworn to destroy the Eldren. This done, of course, it would then turn upon itself again and begin the perpetual squabbling, the constant warring that its peculiar destiny decreed for it.

And yet—should I not, at least, attempt to make the compromise?

Or should I continue with my original ambition, destroy the Eldren, let the race resume its fratricidal sport? In a way it seemed to me that, while some Eldren lived, the race might hold together. If the common enemy remained, at least some sort of unity would exist in the Human Kingdoms. It seemed critical to me then that some Eldren be spared—for the sake of Humanity.

I suddenly realised that there was no contradiction in my loyalties at all. What I had thought was contradictory was, in fact, two halves of a whole. The dream had merely helped me unite them and see everything clearly.

Perhaps this was a complex piece of rationalization. I shall never know. I feel that I was right, though it is possible that subsequent events proved me wrong. At least I tried.

I sat up in my bed as a servant came in with water for me to wash and my own clothes freshly laundered. I washed, dressed myself and when a knock came at the door I called out for the person to enter.

It was Ermizhad. She brought me my breakfast and set it on the table. I thanked her and she looked at me oddly.

"You seem to have changed since last night," she said. "You seem more at one with yourself."

"I think I am," I told her as I ate. "I had another dream last night."

"Was it as terrifying as the others?"

"More terrifying in certain aspects," I said. "But it did not raise problems, this time. It offered me a solution."

"You feel you can fight better."

"If you like. I think it would be in the interest of my race if we made peace with the Eldren. Or, at least, declared a permanent truce."

"You have realised at last that we offer you no danger."

"On the contrary, it is the very danger you offer that makes *your* survival necessary to my race." I smiled, remembering an old aphorism from somewhere. "If you did not exist, it would be necessary to invent you."

A look of intelligence brightened her face. She smiled, too. "I think I understand you."

"Therefore, I intend to present this conclusion to Queen Iolinda," I said. "I hope to persuade her that it is in our interest to end this war against the Eldren."

"And your terms?"

"I see no need to make terms with you," I said. "We will merely stop fighting and go away."

She laughed. "Will it be so easy?"

I looked squarely at her, deliberated for a moment, and then I shook my head. "Perhaps not. But I must try."

"You have become very rational suddenly, Erekosë. I am glad. Your sleep here did do you some good, then."

"And the Eldren, too, perhaps."

She smiled again. "Perhaps."

"I will return to Necranal as soon as possible and speak with Iolinda."

"And if she agrees, you will marry her?"

I felt weak, then. At last I said: "I must do that. Everything would be negated if I did not. You understand?"

"Entirely," she said and there were tears in her eyes as she smiled.

* * *

Arjavh came in a few minutes later and I told him what I intended to do. He received the news rather more sceptically than Ermizhad.

"You do not think I mean what I say?" I asked him.

He shrugged. "I believe you completely, Erekosë. But I do not think the Eldren will survive."

"What is it? Some disease? Something in you that…?"

He laughed shortly. "No, no. I think you will propose a truce and that the people will not let you make it. Your race will only be satisfied when every Eldren has perished. You said that it is their destiny always to fight. Could it not be that secretly they resent the Eldren because the presence of the Eldren means that they cannot go about their normal activities—I mean by that their fighting amongst themselves? Could this be nothing more than a pause before they wipe us out? And if they do not wipe us out now, they will do it very soon, whether you lead them or no."

"Still, I must try," I said.

"Try by all means. But they'll hold you to your vow, I'm sure."

"Iolinda is intelligent. If she listens to my arguments…"

"She is one of them. I doubt if she will listen. Intelligence has little to do with it. Last night when I pleaded with you, I was not myself—I panicked. I know, really, that there can be no peace."

"I must try."

"I hope you succeed."

Perhaps I had been beguiled by the charms of the Eldren, but I did not think so. I would do my best to bring peace to the wasted land of Mernadin, though it meant I could never see my Eldren friends again—never see Ermizhad.

I put the thought from my head and resolved to dwell upon it no longer.

Then a servant entered the room. My herald, accompanied by several marshals, including Count Roldero, had presented himself outside the gates of Loos Ptokai, half-certain that I had been murdered by the Eldren.

"Only sight of you will reassure them," Arjavh murmured. I agreed and left the room.

I heard the herald calling as I approached the city wall. "We fear that you have been guilty of great treachery. Let us see our master—or his corpse." He paused. "Then we shall know what to do."

Arjavh and I mounted the steps to the battlements and I saw relief in the herald's eyes as he noted I was unharmed.

"I have been talking with Prince Arjavh," I said. "And I have been thinking deeply. Our men are weary beyond endurance and the Eldren are now only a few, with just this city in their possession. We could take Loos Ptokai, but I see no point to it. Let us be generous victors, my marshals. Let us declare a truce."

"A truce, Lord Erekosë!" Count Roldero's eyes widened. "Would you rob us of our ultimate prize? Our final, fierce fulfilment? Our greatest triumph? *Peace!*"

"Yes," I said, "peace. Now go back. Tell our warriors I am safe."

"We can take this city easily, Erekosë," Roldero shouted. "There's no need to talk of peace. We can destroy the Eldren once and for all. Have you succumbed to their cursed enchantments again? Have they beguiled you with their smooth words?"

"No," I said, "it was I who suggested it."

Roldero swung his horse around in disgust.

"Peace!" he spat as he and his comrades headed back to the camp. "Our Champion's gone mad!"

Arjavh rubbed his lips with his finger. "Already, I see, there is trouble."

"They fear me," I told him, "and they'll obey me. They'll obey me—for a while, at least."

"Let us hope so," he said.

∽ 24 ∾

THE PARTING

THIS TIME THERE were no cheering crowds in Necranal to welcome me, for news of my mission had gone ahead of me. The people could hardly believe it but where they did believe it, they disapproved. I had shown weakness, in their eyes.

I had not seen Iolinda, of course, since she had become queen. She had a haughty look now as she strode about her throne room, awaiting me.

Privately I was a little amused. I felt like the man who, as an old rejected suitor, returns to see the object of his passion married and become a shrew. I was, therefore, somewhat relieved.

It was a small relief.

"Well, Erekosë," she said. "I know why you are here—why you have forsaken your troops, gone against your word to me that you would destroy every Eldren. Katorn has told me."

"Katorn is here?"

"He came here as soon as he heard your pronouncement from the battlements of Loos Ptokai, where you stood with your Eldren friends."

"Iolinda," I said urgently. "I am convinced that the Eldren are weary of war, that they never intended to threaten the Two

Continents at all. They want only peace."

"Peace we shall have. When the Eldren race has perished."

"Iolinda, if you love me, you will listen to me, at least."

"If *I* love *you*? And what of the Lord Erekosë? Does he still love his queen?"

I opened my mouth, but I could not speak.

And suddenly there were tears in her eyes. "Oh, Erekosë." Her tone softened. "Can it be true?"

"No," I said thickly. "I still love you, Iolinda. We are to be married."

But she knew. She had suspected; but now she knew. However, if peace could result from my action, I was still prepared to pretend, to lie, to declare my passion for her, to marry her.

"I still want to marry you, Iolinda," I said.

"No," she said. "No. You do not."

"I will," I said desperately. "If peace with the Eldren comes about…"

Again her wide eyes blazed. "You insult me, my lord. Not on those terms, Erekosë. Never. You are guilty of high treason against us. The people already speak of you as a traitor."

"But I conquered a continent for them. I took Mernadin."

"All but Loos Ptokai—where your wanton Eldren bitch waits for you."

"Iolinda! That is not true!"

But it was almost true.

"You are unfair…" I began.

"And you are a traitor! Guards!"

As if they had been prepared for this, a dozen of the Imperial Guards rushed in, led by their captain, Lord Katorn. There was a hint of triumph in his eyes and then I knew for certain that he had always hated me because he desired Iolinda.

And I knew, whether I drew my sword or not, he would slay me where I stood.

So I drew my sword. The sword Kanajana. It glowed and the glow was reflected in Katorn's black eyes.

"Take him, Katorn!" cried Iolinda. And her voice was a scream of agony. I had betrayed her. I had failed to be the strength she needed so desperately. "Take him. Alive or dead. He is a traitor to his kind!"

I was a traitor to her. That was what she really meant. That was why I must die.

But I still hoped to save something. "It is untrue…" I began. But Katorn was already cautiously advancing, his men spreading out behind him. I backed to a wall, near a window. The throne room was on the first storey of the palace. Outside were the private gardens of the queen. "Think, Iolinda," I said. "Retract your command. You are driven by jealousy. I'm no traitor."

"*Slay him, Katorn!*"

But I slew Katorn. As he came rushing at me, my sword flicked across his writhing, hate-filled face. He screamed, staggered, his hands rushed up to his head and then he toppled in his golden armour, toppled and fell with a crash to the flagstones.

He was the first human I was to slay.

The other guards came on, but more warily. I fought off their blades, slew a couple more, drove the others back, glimpsed Queen Iolinda watching me, her eyes full of tears, and leaped to the sill of the window.

"Goodbye, Queen. You have lost your champion now."

I jumped.

I landed in a rosebush that ripped at my skin, broke free and ran towards the gate of the garden, the guards behind me.

I tore the gate open and rushed down the hill and into the twisting streets of Necranal, with the guards in pursuit, their ranks joined by a howling pack of citizens who had no idea why I was wanted or even who I was. They chased me for the sheer pleasure of the hunt. My situation reflected more than ever the perpetual paradox of my life since I had obeyed Humanity's summons. Not long since I had led them. I had been the most powerful man in the world. And now, suddenly, I was a fugitive, running through the streets like a common pickpocket.

So it was thus that things turned. Iolinda's pain and jealousy had clouded her mind. And soon her decision would be the cause of more bloodshed than even she had demanded.

I ran, blindly at first, and then towards the river. My crew, I hoped, would still be loyal to me. If they were, then there was a faint chance of escape. I gained the ship just before my pursuers. I leaped aboard screaming:

"Prepare to sail!"

Only half the crew was aboard. The rest was on shore, in the taverns, but those remaining hurriedly shipped out the oars while we held the guards and the citizens at bay.

Then we shoved off and began our hasty flight down the Droonaa River.

It was some time before they managed to commandeer a ship for pursuit and by that time we were safely outdistancing them. My crew asked no questions. They were used to my silences, my actions which sometimes seemed peculiar. But, a week after we were on course over the sea, bound for Mernadin, I told them briefly that I was now an outlaw.

"Why, Lord Erekosë?" asked my captain. "It seems unjust."

"It is unjust, I think. Call it the queen's malice. I suspect Katorn spoke against me, making her hate me."

They were satisfied with the explanation and, when we put in at a small cove near the Plains of Melting Ice, I bade them farewell, mounted my horse and rode swiftly for Loos Ptokai, knowing not what I should do when I got there. Knowing only that I must let Arjavh know the turn events had taken.

He had been right. Humanity would not let me show mercy.

My crew bid me farewell with a certain amount of affection. They did not know—and neither did I—that they were soon to be killed because of me.

Now I crept into Loos Ptokai. I sneaked through the great siege camp that we had constructed there and, at night, entered the city of the Eldren.

Arjavh rose from his bed when he heard I had returned.

"Well, Erekosë?" He looked searchingly at me. Then he said: "You were not successful, were you? You have been riding hard and you have been fighting. What happened?"

I told him.

He sighed. "Well, our advice was foolish. Now you will die when we die."

"I would rather that, I think," I said.

Two months passed. Two ominous months in Loos Ptokai. Humanity did not attack the city immediately and it soon emerged that they were awaiting orders from Queen Iolinda. She, it appeared, had refused to make a decision.

The inaction was oppressive in itself.

I fretted often at the battlements, looking out over the great camp and wishing that the thing would start and be finished. Only Ermizhad eased my unhappiness. We openly acknowledged our love now.

And because I loved her, I began to want to save her.

I wanted to save her and I wanted to save myself and I wanted to save all the Eldren in Loos Ptokai, for I wanted to stay with Ermizhad for ever. I did not want to be destroyed.

Desperately I tried to think of ways in which we could defeat that great force, but every plan I made was a wild one and could not work.

And then, one day, I remembered a conversation I had had with Arjavh on the plateau after he had defeated me in battle.

I went looking for him and found him in his study. He was reading from one of the beautifully decorated Eldren scrolls.

"Erekosë? Are they beginning their attack?"

"No, Arjavh. But I recall that you told me once about some ancient weapons your race had—that you still have."

"What?"

"The old terrible weapons," I said. "The ones you swore never to use again because they could destroy so much!"

He shook his head. "Not those."

"Use them this once, Arjavh," I begged him. "Make a show of strength, that is all. They will be ready to discuss peace then."

He rolled up his scroll. "No. They will never discuss peace with us. They would rather die. I do not think that even this situation merits the breaking of that ancient vow."

"Arjavh," I said. "I respect the reasons for refusing to use the weapons. But I have grown to love the Eldren. I have already broken one vow. Let me break another—for you. "

He still shook his head.

"Just agree to this, then," I said. "If the time comes when I feel we could use them, will you let me decide—take the decision out of your hands, make it my responsibility?"

He looked searchingly at me. The orbless eyes seemed to pierce me.

"Perhaps," he said.

"Arjavh—will you?"

"We Eldren have never been motivated as much by self-interest as you humans—and never to the extent of destroying another race, Erekosë. Do not confuse our values with those of mankind."

"I am not," I replied. "That is my reason for asking you this. I could not bear to see your noble race perish at the hands of those beasts beyond our walls!"

Arjavh stood up and replaced the scroll in the shelves. "Iolinda spoke the truth," he said quietly. "You are a traitor to your own race."

"'Race' is a meaningless term. It was you and Ermizhad who told me to be an individual. I have chosen my loyalties."

He pursed his lips. "Well…"

"I seek only to stop them continuing in their folly," I said.

He clenched his thin, pale hands together.

"Arjavh. I asked you because of the love I have for Ermizhad and the love she has for me. Because of the great friendship you have given me. For all Eldren left alive, I beg you to let me take the decision if it becomes necessary."

"For Ermizhad?" He raised his slanting eyebrows. "For you? For me? For my people? Not for revenge?"

"No," I said quietly. "I do not think so."

"Very well. I leave the decision to you. I suppose that is fair. I do not want to die. But remember—do not act as unwisely as others of your kind."

"I will not," I promised.

I think I kept that particular promise.

25

THE ATTACK

AND THE DAYS continued to pass. Gradually the air began to chill; night came sooner. Winter threatened. If winter arrived before Count Roldero, we would be safe until spring, for the invaders would be fools to attempt a heavy siege.

They realised this, too, and it seemed Iolinda must have come to a decision. She gave them permission to attack Loos Ptokai.

After much bickering among themselves, I learned, the marshals elected one of themselves, the most experienced, to act as their war champion.

They elected Count Roldero.

The siege commenced in earnest.

Their massive siege engines were brought forward, including the giant cannon known as the Firedrakes—great black things of iron, decorated with fierce reliefs.

Roldero rode up and his herald announced his presence. I went to speak with him from the battlements.

"Greetings, Erekosë the Traitor!" he called. "We have decided to punish you—and all the Eldren within these walls. We would have slaughtered the Eldren cleanly, but now we intend to put to slow death all those we capture."

I was saddened.

"Roldero, Roldero," I begged. "We were friends once. You were perhaps the only true friend I had. We drank together and fought together, made jokes together. We were comrades, Roldero. Good comrades."

His horse fidgeted beneath him, pawing at the earth.

"That was an age ago," he said without looking up at me.

"Little more than a year, Roldero."

"But we are not those two friends any longer, Erekosë." He looked up, shielding his eyes with a gauntleted hand. I saw that his face had grown old and it bore many new scars. Doubtless I looked as changed as he. "We are different men," Roldero said, and wrenching at his reins drove his horse away, digging his long spurs savagely into its flanks. Now there was nothing we could do but fight.

The Firedrakes boomed and their solid shot slammed against the walls. Blazing fireballs from captured Eldren artillery (we had become less fastidious as the war went on) screamed over the walls and into the streets. These were followed by thousands of arrows that came in a black shower, blotting out the light.

And then a million men rushed against our handful of defenders.

We replied with what cannon we had, but we relied mainly on archers to meet that first wave, for we were short of shot.

And we repelled them. After ten hours of fighting they fell back.

Then, next day and the day after, they continued to attack. But Loos Ptokai, the ancient capital of Mernadin, held firm.

Battalion upon battalion of yelling warriors mounted the siege towers and we again replied with arrows, with molten metal and, economically, with the fire-spewing cannon of the Eldren. We fought bravely, Arjavh and I leading the defenders and, whenever they sighted me, the warriors of Humanity screamed for vengeance and died striving for the privilege of slaying me.

We fought side by side, like brothers, Arjavh and I, but our Eldren warriors were tiring and, after a week of constant barrage, we began to realise that we could not much longer hold back that tide of steel.

That night we sat together after Ermizhad had gone to bed. We massaged our aching muscles and we spoke little.

Then I said: "We shall all be dead soon, Arjavh. You and I. Ermizhad. The rest of your folk."

He continued to dig his fingers into his shoulder, kneading it to loosen it. "Yes," he said. "Soon."

I wanted him to raise the subject that was on the tip of my tongue, but he would not.

The next day, scenting our defeat, the warriors of Humanity came at us with greater vigour than ever. The Firedrakes were brought in closer and began steadily to bombard the main gates.

I saw Roldero, mounted on his great black horse, directing the operation and there was something about his stance that made me realise that he was sure he would break our defences that day.

I turned to Arjavh, who stood beside me on the wall, and I was about to speak when several of the Firedrakes boomed in unison. The black metal shook, the shot screamed from their snouts, hit the main gates, which were of metal, and split the left one down the middle. It did not fall, but it was so badly weakened that one more cannonade would bring it completely down.

"Arjavh!" I yelled. "We must break out the old weapons. We must arm the Eldren!"

His face was pale, but he shook his head.

"Arjavh! We must! Another hour and we'll be driven off these battlements! Another three and we'll be overwhelmed entirely!"

He looked to where Roldero was directing the cannoneers and this time he did not remonstrate. He nodded. "Very well. I agreed that you would decide. Come."

He led me down the steps.

I only hoped he had not overestimated their power.

Arjavh led me to the vaults that lay at the core of the city. We moved along bare corridors of polished black marble, lighted by small bulbs which burned with a greenish glow. We came to a door of dark metal and he pressed a stud beside it. The door moved open and we entered an elevator which bore us yet farther downwards.

I was again astonished at the Eldren. They had deliberately given up all these marvels to satisfy their ideals of justice and honour.

Then we stepped into a great hall full of weirdly wrought machines that looked as if they had just been manufactured. They stretched for nearly half a mile ahead of us.

"These are the weapons," said Arjavh bleakly.

Around the high walls were arranged handguns of various kinds; there were rifles and objects that looked to John Daker's eye like anti-tank weapons. There were squat war machines on caterpillar treads, with glass cabins and couches for a single man to lie flat upon and operate the controls. I was surprised that there were no flying machines of any kind—or none that I recognised as such. I mentioned this to Arjavh.

"Flying machines! It would be interesting if such things could be invented. But I do not think it is possible. We have never, in all our history, been able to develop a machine that will safely stay in the air for any length of time."

I was amazed at this odd gap in their technology, but I commented on it no further.

"Now you have seen these fierce things," he said, "do you still feel you should use them?"

He doubtless thought such weapons were not familiar to me. They were not so very different to the war machines John Daker had known. And, in my dreams, I had seen much stranger weapons.

"Let us ready them," I said to him.

We returned to the surface and there instructed our warriors to transport the weapons to the surface.

Roldero had smashed in one of our gates now and we had had to bring up cannon to defend it, but the warriors of Humanity were beginning to press in and some hand-to-hand fighting was going on at the approach to the gates.

Night was falling. I hoped that, in spite of their gain, the human army would retreat at dark and give us the time we needed. Through the gap in the gate I saw Roldero urging his men in. Doubtless he hoped to consolidate his advantage before the twilight ended.

I ordered more men to the breach.

Already I was beginning to doubt my own decision.

Perhaps Arjavh was right and it was criminal to let the power of the ancient weapons loose. But then, I thought, what does it matter? Better destroy them and half the planet than let them destroy the beauty that was the Eldren.

I was forced to smile at this reaction in myself. Arjavh would not have approved of it. Such a thought was alien to him.

I saw Roldero bring in more men to counter our forces and I swung into the saddle of a nearby horse, spurring it towards the crucial breach.

I drew my poison sword, Kanajana, and I voiced my battle-cry—the battle-cry that only a short while ago had urged these warriors I attacked into battle against those I now led. They heard it and, as I suspected, were disconcerted.

I leaped my horse over the heads of my own men and confronted Roldero. He looked at me in astonishment and pulled his horse up short.

"Would you fight me, Roldero?" I said.

He shrugged. "Aye. I'll fight you, traitor."

And he rushed at me with his reins looped over his arm and both hands around the hilt of his great sword. It whistled over my head as I ducked.

Everywhere about us, beneath the broken walls of Loos Ptokai, human and Eldren fought desperately in the fading light.

Roldero was tired, more tired than I was, but he battled valiantly on and I could not get through his guard. His sword caught me a blow on my helmet and I reeled and struck back and caught *him* on the helmet. My helmet stayed on, but his was half-pulled off. He wrenched it off all the way and flung it aside. His hair had turned completely white since I had last seen him bareheaded.

His face was flushed and his eyes bright, his lips drawn back over his teeth. He tried to stab his sword through my visor, but I ducked under the blow and he fell forward in his saddle and I brought up my sword and drove it down into his breastbone.

He groaned and then his face lost all its anger and he gasped: "Now we can be friends again, Erekosë…" and he died.

I looked down at him as he collapsed over the neck of his horse. I remembered his kindness, the wine he had brought me to help me sleep, the advice he had tried to give me. And I remembered him pushing the dead king from his saddle. Yet, Count Roldero was a good man, a good man forced by history to do evil. By his own rule he had been condemned.

His black horse turned and began to canter back towards the count's distant pavilion.

I raised my sword in salute and then shouted to the humans

who fought on. "Look, warriors of Humanity! Look! Your war champion is defeated!"

The sun was setting.

The warriors began to withdraw, looking at me in hatred as I laughed at them, but not daring to attack me while the bloody sword Kanajana was in my hand.

One of them did call back, however.

"We are not leaderless, Erekosë, if that is what you think. We have the queen to send us into battle. She has come to be witness to your destruction tomorrow!"

Iolinda was with the besiegers!

I thought swiftly and then yelled: "Tell your mistress to come tomorrow to our walls. Come at dawn to parley!"

Through the night we worked to reinforce the gate and to position the new-found weapons. They were raised wherever they would fit and the Eldren soldiers were armed with the hand weapons.

I wondered if Iolinda would get the message and, if she did get it, whether she would deign to come.

She came. She came with her remaining marshals in all their proud panoply of war. That panoply seemed so insignificant now, against the power of the ancient Eldren weapons.

We had set one of the new cannon pointing up at the sky so that we could demonstrate its fearful potential.

Iolinda's voice drifted up to us.

"Greetings, Eldren—and greetings to your human lapdog. Is he a well-trained pet now?"

"Greetings, Iolinda," I said, showing my face. "You begin to show your father's penchant for poor insults and obvious irony. Let's waste no further time."

"I am already wasting time," she said. "We are going to destroy you all today."

"Perhaps not," I said. "For we offer you a truce—and peace."

Iolinda laughed aloud. "*You* offer us peace, traitor! You should be begging for peace—though you'll get none!"

"I warn you, Iolinda," I shouted desperately. "I warn you all. We have fresh weapons—weapons which once came near to destroying this whole Earth! Watch!"

I gave the order to fire the giant cannon.

An Eldren warrior depressed a stud on the controls.

There came a humming from the cannon and all at once a tremendous blinding bolt of golden energy gouted from its snout. The heat alone blistered our skins and we fell back, shielding our eyes.

Horses shrieked and reared. The marshals' faces were grey and their mouths gaped. They fought to control their mounts. Only Iolinda sat firmly in her saddle, apparently calm.

"That is what we offer you if you will not have peace," I shouted. "We have a dozen like it and there are others that are different, but as powerful, and we have hand cannon which can kill a hundred men at a sweep. What say you now?"

Iolinda raised her face and stared directly up at me.

"We fight," she said.

"Iolinda," I pleaded. "For our old love, for your own sake—do not fight. We will not harm you. You can go home, all of you, and live in security for the rest of your lives. I mean it."

"Security!" She laughed bitterly. "Security, while such weapons as these exist!"

"You must believe me, Iolinda!"

"No," she said. "Humanity will fight to the end and, because the Good One favours us, doubtless we will win. We are pledged to wage war on sorcery and there was never greater sorcery than what we have seen today."

"It is not sorcery. It is science. It is only like your cannon, but more powerful."

"Sorcery!" Everyone was murmuring it now. They were like savages, these fools.

"If we continue to fight," I said, "it will be a fight to the finish. The Eldren would prefer to let you go, once this battle is won. But if we win, I intend to clean the planet of your kind, just as you swore you would do to the Eldren. Take the chance. A peace! Be sane."

"We will die by sorcery," she said, "if we have to. But we will die fighting it."

I was too weary to continue. "Then let us finish this business," I told her.

Iolinda wheeled her horse away and, with her marshals in her wake, galloped back to order the attack.

I did not see Iolinda perish. There were so many that perished that day.

They came and we met them. They were helpless against our weapons. Energy spouted from the guns and seared into their ranks. How quickly they fell and how tragically they died. We all felt sorrow as we let loose the howling waves of force which swept across them and destroyed them, turning proud men and beasts to blackened rubble.

We did as they had predicted we would do. We destroyed them all.

I pitied them as they came on, the cream of Humanity's menfolk. Each wave was burned down as soon as it came within two hundred yards of our walls. We begged them to retreat. They came again. I began to guess that they wished to die. They sought rest in death.

It took two hours to destroy a million warriors.

* * *

When the extermination was over, I was filled with a strange emotion which I could not then and cannot now define. It was a mixture of grief, relief and triumph. I mourned for Iolinda. She was somewhere there in the heap of blackened bone and smouldering flesh—one piece of ruined meat amongst many, her beauty gone in the same instant as her life.

And it was then that I made my final decision. Or did I, indeed, make it at all? Was it not what I had been brought here to do?

Or was it the crime I had mentioned earlier? Was this the crime I committed that doomed me to be what I was?

Was I right?

In spite of Arjavh's constant antagonism to my plan, I ordered the machines out of Loos Ptokai and, mounted in one of them, led them overland.

This is what I did:

Two months before, I had been responsible for winning the cities of Mernadin for Humanity. Now I reclaimed them in the name of the Eldren.

I reclaimed them in a terrible way. I destroyed every human being occupying them.

A week and we were at Paphanaal, where the fleets of mankind lay at anchor in the great harbour.

I destroyed those fleets as I destroyed the garrison—men, women and children perished. None was spared.

And then, for many of the machines were amphibious, I led the Eldren across the sea to the Two Continents, though Arjavh and Ermizhad were not with me.

These cities fell: Noonos of the jewel-studded towers fell. Tarkar fell. The wondrous cities of the wheatlands, Stalaco, Calodemia, Mooros and Ninadoon, all fell. Wedmah, Shilaal, Sinaan and others fell, crumbling in an inferno of gouting energy. They fell in a few moments.

In Necranal, the pastel-coloured city of the mountain, five million citizens died and all that was left of Necranal was the scorched, smoking mountain itself.

But I was thorough. Not merely the great cities were destroyed. Villages were destroyed. Hamlets were destroyed. Towns and farms were destroyed.

I found some people hiding in caves. The caves were destroyed.

I destroyed forests where they might flee. I destroyed the very stones they might creep under.

I would doubtless have destroyed every blade of grass if Arjavh had not come hurrying over the ocean to stop me.

He was horrified at what I had done. He begged me to stop.

I stopped.

There was no more killing to do.

We made our way back to the coast and we paused to look at the smouldering mountainside that had been Necranal.

"For one woman's wrath," said Prince Arjavh, "and another's love, you did this?"

I shrugged. "I do not know. I think I did it for the only kind of peace that will last. I know my race too well. This Earth would have been for ever rent by strife of some kind. I had to decide who best deserved to live. If they had destroyed the Eldren, they would have soon turned on each other, as you know. And they fight for such empty things, too. For power over their fellows, for a bauble, for an extra acre of land that they will not till, for possession of a woman who doesn't want them."

"You decided that! You took this vast responsibility onto your own shoulders? You judged them and executed them according to your own interpretation of justice?" Arjavh said quietly. "Really, Erekosë, I do not think you know yet what you have done."

I sighed. "But it is done," I said.

"Yes." His eyes were full of a profound pity for me. He gripped my arm. "Come, friend. Back to Mernadin. Leave this stink behind. Ermizhad awaits you."

I was an empty man, then, bereft of emotion. I followed him towards the river. It moved sluggishly now. It was choked with black dust, with burned flesh.

"I think I did right," I said. "It was not my will, you know, but something else. I think it might have been my fate from the beginning. I think it was another will than mine which dragged me here—not Rigenos. Rigenos, like me, was a puppet—a tool used, as I was used. It was preordained that Humanity should die on this planet."

"It is better that you think that," he said. "Come now. Let us go home."

❧ EPILOGUE ❧

THE SCARS OF that destruction have healed now, as I end my chronicle.

I returned to Loos Ptokai to wed Ermizhad, to have the Eldren secret of immortality conferred upon me, to brood for a year or two until my brain cleared.

It is clear now. I feel no guilt for what I did. I feel more certain than ever that it was not my decision.

Perhaps that is madness? Perhaps I have rationalised my guilt? If so, I am at one with my madness, it does not tear me in two as my dreams used to. I have those dreams rarely these days.

So we are here, the three of us—Ermizhad, Arjavh and I. Arjavh is undisputed ruler of the Earth, an Eldren Earth, and we rule with him.

We cleansed this Earth of humankind. I am its last representative. And in so doing I feel that we knitted this planet back into the pattern, allowed it to drift, at last, harmoniously with a harmonious universe. For the universe is old, perhaps even older than I, and it could not tolerate the humans who broke its peace.

Did I do right?

You must judge for yourself, wherever you are.

For me, it is too late to ask that question. I have sufficient control nowadays never to ask it. The only way in which I could answer it would involve destroying my own sanity.

One thing puzzles me. If, indeed, Time is cyclic, in some manner, and the universe we know will be born again to turn another long cycle, then Humanity will one day arise again, somehow, on this Earth and my adopted people will disappear from the Earth, or seem to.

And if you are human who reads this, perhaps you know. Perhaps my question seems naïve and you are at this moment laughing at me. But I have no answer. I can imagine none.

I am not to be the father of your race, human, for Ermizhad and I cannot produce children.

Then how shall you come again to disrupt the harmony of the universe?

And will I be here to receive you? Will I become your hero again or will I die with the Eldren fighting you?

Or will I die before then and be the leader who brings disrupting Humanity to Earth? I cannot say.

Which of the names will I have next time you call?

Now Earth is peaceful. The silent air carries only the sounds of quiet laughter, the murmur of conversation, the small noises of small animals. We and Earth are at peace.

But how long can it last?

Oh, how long can it last?

ABOUT THE AUTHOR

BORN IN LONDON in 1939, Michael Moorcock now lives in Texas. A prolific and award-winning writer with more than eighty works of fiction and non-fiction to his name, he is the creator of Elric, Jerry Cornelius and Colonel Pyat, amongst many other memorable characters. In 2008, *The Times* named Moorcock in their list of "The 50 greatest British writers since 1945".